Books by Clark Blaise

A North American Education (1973)

Tribal Justice (1974)

Days and Nights in Calcutta (1977)
(with Bharati Mukherjee)

Lunar Attractions (1979)

Lusts (1983)

Resident Alien (1986)

The Sorrow and the Terror (1987)
(with Bharati Mukherjee)

Man and His World (1992)

I Had a Father (1993)

Here, There and Everywhere:
Lectures on Australian, Canadian, American and Post-Modern Writing (1994)

If I Were Me (1997)

Southern Stories (2000)

Time Lord:
The Remarkable Canadian Who Missed His Train (2001)

The Selected Stories of

CLARK BLAISE

Volume Two

Pittsburgh Stories

With an Introduction by
Robert Boyers

The Porcupine's Quill

NATIONAL LIBRARY OF CANADA CATALOGUING IN PUBLICATION DATA

Blaise, Clark, 1940–
The selected stories of Clark Blaise

Introduction to v. 2 by Robert Boyers.
Contents: v. 1. Southern stories – v. 2. Pittsburgh stories.
ISBN 0-88984-219-1 (v. 1). – ISBN 0-88984-227-2 (v. 2).

I. Title.   II. Title: Southern stories.   III. Title: Pittsburgh stories.

PS8553.L34S45 2000   C813'.54   C00-932402-X
PR9199.3.B52S45 2000

Published by The Porcupine's Quill,
68 Main Street, Erin, Ontario NOB 1TO.
www.sentex.net/~pql

Readied for the press by John Metcalf; copy edited by Doris Cowan.
Typeset in Minion, printed on Zephyr Antique laid,
and bound at the Porcupine's Quill Inc.

Represented in Canada by the Literary Press Group.
Trade orders are available from General Distribution Services.

We acknowledge the support of the Ontario Arts Council,
and the Canada Council for the Arts for our publishing program.
The financial support of the Government of Canada
through the Book Publishing Industry Development Program
is also gratefully acknowledged.

1   2   3   4   ·   03   02   01

Canada

Contents

Introduction

The narrator of Clark Blaise's story 'Identity' describes a life 'of sharp and inexplicable and unmendable breaks', a life 'without completion' and, in that sense at least, much like the lives of the other protagonists in Blaise's *Pittsburgh Stories*. These are, for the most part, coming-of-age stories in which no one quite develops or advances in the accredited way, stories permeated by an air of obstruction and regret. Everywhere the will to explain and understand is confronted by the sheer, recalcitrant, unlovely obstinacy of the world. Even the familiar assumes, in Blaise's stories, the status of the 'off plumb', the 'slightly skewed'. Reality itself, for Blaise's characters, is more than a little problematic, so that 'concept' and 'theory' and 'myth', however vague or unreliable, are inevitably invoked as alternative, if hopelessly inadequate, ways to think about the truth, ever seductive, ever out of reach.

Even place is problematic in Blaise's work, 'Pittsburgh' being at once a set of physical coordinates and a state of mind prompting characters to dream of an impossible, lost, beckoning *someplace else*. Often the *other* place is a Europe remembered or read about, but it is just as likely to be an even more remote *someplace* – 'anything that spoke of vast distance and remote time. Realities other than the South Side of Pittsburgh,' says the character in 'Sitting Shivah with Cousin Benny', 'earned my traitor's allegiance.'

All the same, Blaise's Pittsburgh is not entirely without its charms. Occasionally there is nostalgia for the 'real' Pittsburgh where the working-class or defeated Blaise protagonists cannot afford to live, the 'East End' Pittsburgh of the genteel Carnegie Museum where on weekends a boy 'sketched the animals and skeletons, then walked across the parking lot to Forbes Field to take advantage of free admission to Pirates' games after the seventh inning.' There are, in addition, nostalgias associated with the Pittsburgh of Willa Cather, Kenneth Burke and Malcolm Cowley, a mythic city where conversation bristles with ideas

7

and the provincial has been permanently banished. But that Pittsburgh is rarely accessible to the hungry imagination of Blaise's youthful protagonists, and the longing for yet more remote, alien worlds is never far from the surface even in the more optimistic stories.

It is tempting, of course, to account for the inexorable attraction to otherness by citing the facts of Blaise's peripatetic, cross-border, U.S.–Canadian life. This is a man, after all, who has been identified with several locales, who entitled one of his mixed-genre, semi-autobiographical books *Resident Alien,* who has seemed, in the words of Fenton Johnson, always 'of and apart from the country of which he writes.' And yet the resort to biography, to Blaise's wanderlust and mixed Canadian-American identity, here seems just a little too easy. Blaise, after all, has been deeply invested in the places he writes about. It is not as if he offers to us in his stories mere tourist inventories of the American South, or Montreal, or Pittsburgh. In stories like 'Dunkelblau' we can see the numbers on the Pittsburgh trolleys, smell the 'acrid fumes', hear 'the coughs and page-shufflings of the white-haired men and women' in the public library, with its 'six-storey ceiling' and 'polished wood'. The men coming home from work in Blaise's stories of the forties and fifties are 'sooty, sweating', the buildings 'smoke-blackened'. On clear days, 'a rarity in Pittsburgh in those years, [you] can see through the blackened branches to the top of the Gulf Building.' A woman keeping house finds that, because of the pervasive soot, she has to launder the white curtains every week.

Nor is the detail merely a matter of local colour. Blaise's characters move through Pittsburgh and its environs alert to its class conflicts and its baulked ambitions, its 'Hunkie and Polack origins', its gilded age and its status as 'the dirtiest city in America, with the ugliest history'. The desire to escape or at least to dream of escape is matched in intensity by a compensatory sense of reality, of a place with palpable claims on one's imagination, if not on one's loyalty. The Jewish names on the Pittsburgh Pirates' 1950s roster, intoned one after the other in 'Sitting Shivah with Cousin Benny', constitute an inescapable token of intimacy, involvement. 'They were "our boys",' the narrator concedes, though he is not a Jew, and he understands entirely when his Jewish uncle asks, 'What are we running, a *schlimazel* farm? Too many of our boys on the field, not enough in the front office.' The world of this boy's childhood is not alien, not at all what some have described as an outsider's 'placeless place' in a 'timeless time'.

No doubt there are mysteries and gaps in Blaise's several worlds, missing facts that make his Prairie towns, or his Southland, or his Pittsburgh sometimes seem a mere way station on a journey to a world elsewhere or an allegorical condition to which meanings may be cautiously affixed. Blaise's Pittsburgh, circa 1952, or 1960, can seem almost too real, too mundane, too entirely irredeemable, so that it exists for us principally as that which had simply to be left behind, grown out of, if any human progress was to be accomplished. For one adult character, Pittsburgh is the not-Germany, the place where the 'English equivalents' of German words or names will never be 'satisfactory'. For another character, stories of Europe, even of a Europe ravaged by war and human disaster, are always 'more attractive than anything I knew in Pittsburgh', where the best you can do is survey the damage and think about the blandness of the standard domestic routine. For such characters, what is missing in their present, fallen world may well be unnameable, but it darkens their sense of possibility and inspires in them a tendency to look for portents, to read everything as if it were a sign of something else. Characters for whom the present landscape is never enough are in Blaise preternaturally hungry for meaning, though they mistrust even their own domestic tales and rarely forgive themselves their own lapses in 'perception', their inability to come up with impeccably convincing, perfectly coherent narratives. If *Europe* is the name of their desire, or *Mozart*, or *art*, they know all the same that they belong to the makeshift and provisional, the forever diminished and diminishing Pittsburgh, or Dakota, or Moscow 'of dreadful *Nyet*', that for them Europe can never be more than the polish, the poise, the confidence *that is not*.

One feels in all of this no trace of a merely theoretical anguish, no deliberately portentous assembling of darkly telling anecdotes to confirm the resolutely downward drift of a settled disposition. Blaise's facts and metaphors proliferate like washes of colour saturating a canvas that has been primed to absorb them, but much of the colour is significant for the mood it imparts rather than for any point it may be said to underline. Just so, the images in Blaise often carry a powerful charge, but they are, with rare exception, 'passing, irretrievable', as one character registers them. Even where the smell of apocalypse is in the air, the imagery mostly bespeaks a gradual decline, what is once called an 'implicit savagery' or, elsewhere, a 'long disenchantment'. There are no grand disclosures in Blaise, though there are small shocks, and the language, for all its occasional bluntness and its resistance to languor or meander, gathers its effects patiently, with a special feeling for the lures and deceptions that make any prospect of disclosure seem both appealing and improbable.

If 'Identity' is the most powerful story in a volume of unfailingly nervy fictions, its power has much to do with the multiple betrayals that give the story its shape and its motive. Identity itself, in this story, as in others by Blaise, is a species of betrayal, an insidious fiction governed by the specious idea that one may realistically aspire to wholeness even as one may reasonably believe 'you can be anything you want to be.' The boy in Blaise's story is ever in pursuit of *what* and *why* and *who*. Though he observes and reflects, he remains uncertain about everything. Even his love for his father, never in doubt, is compromised, threatened, by his inability to know precisely what kind of man his father is. 'He'd been married twice before, so far as I knew,' the boy says, 'and I'd found that out only when I overheard it. It didn't seem safe to ask if he had other children.' Why didn't it 'seem safe to ask?' Presumably because the answer to such a question would itself be unreliable, and might therefore open up additional questions, similarly provocative and disturbing. No doubt the inability to know with anything like confidence is related, in Blaise's story, to the hunger for comforting fictions that might correct the pervasive sense of betrayal or misgiving. But the comforting fictions in 'Identity' do not soothe. The desire to be 'normal', to grow up without dark misgiving, is routinely confronted by the disorderly procession of intimations that say, unmistakably, no, not simple, not soothing, not ever clear.

For all the gathering force of inevitability in 'Identity', for all the accumulating evidence to suggest that identity itself will remain for Blaise's central character unknowable, there is a good deal of comic surprise and inflection. Though the transparently fragile, obviously constructed 'sheltering memories of childhood' are relentlessly dismantled in the story, the boy seems often amused even by the more lurid aspects of the painful process. 'There wasn't a time I visited,' he tells us of his frequent forays to a friend's apartment, 'when his mother ['something lurid', 'her habits and language loose and leering', 'her entire stock of lingerie and negligees ... usually on display'] was up and moving that I didn't come out of that apartment with something shocking to me, some hunk of flesh observed or knowledge that would stimulate me like some laboratory rat in an uncontrolled experiment.' The awfulness of the household he visits and the boy's distress at his raw susceptibility to shock and stimulation are here evoked with a mixture of clear-eyed wonder and an emotion bordering on disinterested gratitude. 'She had nothing of the mother in her,' the boy observes, clearly in a position to contrast the behaviour of his friend's mother with the more obviously maternal features of his own, and therefore able to understand something essential he wishes to hold on to. 'To have been the son of such a woman, to have absorbed the full blast without any shield,' he later reflects, again with the relative security of another 'son' who has had many a 'blast' to absorb, but more than one kind of shield to protect him. Not to know things is hard, Blaise suggests, but distress, exasperation, disappointment are somehow bearable when there is some foundation of affection, some normative ideal of decent conduct available to shield one from the full force of the inevitable betrayals and indecencies.

This foundation, the more or less secure presence of a modest, normative ideal, saves Blaise's story from what might otherwise be a fatal tendency to pathos and self-pity. Yes, the boy tells us, everything has its consequences. Awfulness takes its toll. The hunks of unassimilable flesh must eventually, rapidly produce a nervous susceptibility to sexual excitement, even a readiness to regard one's own mother as a sexual being, alluring and forbidden. But such intimations are represented as manageable, though they are never quite mastered or discarded. In this way we understand every aspect of the boy's unhappiness and vulnerability, which he negotiates not with conventional coping mechanisms but with an inchoate instinct for balance, proportion, irony. He may feel, much of the time, helpless, a subject in someone else's experiment, but he is alert to moments of reprieve. Like other Blaise protagonists, his tendency to melancholia, his attunement to defeat, is offset by an acute sense that there must be more to life than melancholy and disappointment. His suffering, like his gift for irony and proportion, is more a mood than a system.

To be sure, grimness often overwhelms irony in Blaise's fiction. 'People wonder,' the epileptic boy in 'Identity' says, 'what it's like to die, and since I've done it several hundred little-bad times and a few great compulsive big-bad times, and have died in other ways, too,' he can tell us precisely what it's like. But there is no bravado in the recitation of 'death' and survival and no restriction of the petit-mal and grand-mal 'dying' to the physical aspects of seizure and fit. Neither is there a deliberately worked-up anguish or melodramatic avidity. In spite of the extremity of the controlling idiom – 'Dying is like this' – the narrative generates a sense of the absurd and improbable. The orchestrated juxtapositions are at once compelling and playful, so that the terrible ('Something terrible is happening') is registered along with the bewilderingly delicious ('Christ, my mother is a *sexy* woman'). There are, to be sure, on all sides, tokens of loss and confusion, but we do not doubt that, for all of the developmental damage, there will be a marginally viable future for the boy who determines to tell us of his dying. The name of this assurance is not, decidedly not, optimism, but it is, surely, a function of his demonstrated detachment – call it partial, call it literary, call it emotional – from the pain and disorientation he wishes us to share, to savour.

The works in *Pittsburgh Stories* were written over the better part of four decades, and published originally in various books and magazines. They are, in important respects, miscellaneous, for all of their common tendency to mix memory and desire, to track the contradictory patterns of tenderness and betrayal in human lives. One feels in them, albeit in varying degrees, a continuous agitation of surface and sympathy. Nothing, it seems, is ever resolved for good and all in these works. For all of their obsession with varieties of blindness and defeat, they do not quite capitulate to nihilism. Characters may surrender to 'the whole sad business', may suppose every avenue of escape closed to them, may doubt their own capacity for renewal. But they are, in their several ways, oddly resilient. Confronted with sure tokens of decline or tawdriness, the Blaise protagonists are never less than incredulous, determined to look further, to wonder, to discover in themselves strange liberties of expression and sentiment. Blaise's feeling for the unaccountable is bracing and vivid, and has nothing to do with the easy mysticism or occultism that provides for many writers of lesser scruple a relief from the problems generated by their own fictions. The *Pittsburgh Stories*, for all of their thoughtfulness about the vicissitudes of identity and the sheer difficulty of knowing, never reach for ostensibly definitive resolutions. Resistant to the joyless as also to the lugubrious and earnest, they are brisk, elegant, intensely human. One hears in them what Thomas Mann called 'the teasing melancholy of the not-yet'.

Robert Boyers

––––––

Robert Boyers is Tisch Professor of Arts and Letters at Skidmore College, editor of the quarterly *Salmagundi* and Director of the New York State Summer Writers Institute. His books include *Atrocity & Amnesia* and *After the Avant-Garde.* He writes regularly on fiction for *The New Republic.*

The Birth of the Blues

As a real young kid, no more than four or five, Frank Keeler wanted recognition for the difficult ideas he was beginning to articulate. The first idea of his life – a truth – was so vivid that it gathered the clouds from the heavens and forced them into a funnel point just over his mother's head. It was Pittsburgh in 1944, and there were dark clouds enough for all the truths of Tolstoy. He was helping his mother to weed their Victory Garden. She was a squat, manly woman with white flabby arms and chin hairs, though she must have been only twenty-nine or thirty that year.

'Sometimes,' he said while working his way down a row of radishes, not knowing what he was pulling until a pinkish bulge in the tuber betrayed him and he quickly tried to replant the evidence – 'sometimes you pull out radishes, I bet, when you're trying to pull out weeds.'

Phrased, it disappointed. What he meant (and remembered meaning) was the darkening of doubt in what had been the bright skies of certainty. It had to do with guilt. Though he was no stranger to the casual butchery of earthworms and caterpillars, this time he had murdered without meaning to. It had to do with a cruelty of nature that the weeds no one wanted looked just like the vegetables that were winning the war and keeping him from being murdered in his bed.

Taken to its extreme, which was the only way he took anything, the equivalence of opposites is a horrible concept.

'Sometimes you sure throw out the baby with the bathwater all right,' his mother joked. Perhaps he hadn't heard properly. It could have been a song or she might have been talking to herself, which she often did. He must have heard it wrong. But she asked again, making no mistake about it, 'That it? The baby with the bathwater?'

From weeds to radishes is natural. Even a child can follow it. From there to moral choice and guilt is a scream for help. Reassurance arrived in the form of a metaphor that he received as literal, wondering if in fact babies were often thrown out with their bathwater; if normal precautions might not reduce, if not eliminate, the number of wet babies squirming in soapy puddles; if mother love might not be invoked on the side of soapy babies everywhere. Obviously, it couldn't be. Luck alone accounted for his survival. An unexpected callousness had been exposed; the world was incredibly brutal. He wanted, for a moment, no part of it. Black clouds were boiling overhead and he thought, Messerschmidts! And he hid his head and held that posture in the rain until his mother pried his arms away.

A freak storm destroyed several small towns just north of Pittsburgh that day.

The configuration was set for life: Dark clouds giving birth to Truth and Destruction; his own contribution dismissed (or worse, rephrased as one of his mother's 'little sayings'). Oh, the dark terrors, the dread that could be rendered by 'from the frying pan into the fire', the swift curtailment of liberty pardoned in 'When in Rome' – all so much bathwater, so much craving for greener grass. The proverbs never quite matched his meaning, never approached the intensity of his premonitions. His mother had been stuffed with sayings and Depression recipes; she was profound on any topic dealing with turnips, disappointment or forbearance.

His father had only one saying: 'Nothing succeeds like success.' He used it when the Pirates were getting pounded by talented opponents who were also getting lucky. It meant that the deck was rigged, either for you or against you. Its analogy was 'The rich get richer.' It was a justification for being poor, for losing, for not trying, for taking what you could get. When Frank got some education years later, he saw it as crude Darwinism.

What can we say about intelligence when the child's highest utterances were clichés even before he formed them? He came to think that his originality would always be blunted on some higher and preexistent logic. Someone would always be there ahead of him. That's how it was and how it would always be; you had to admit you weren't exceptional, you couldn't jump over your mother's sayings, you couldn't invent new clichés.

Years later, he read Hamlet. The melancholy Dane struck him as no hero, basically a winner, one of the rich and gifted, who was mildly incompetent with his tools. Keeler's hero was, alas, Polonius. A man elevated by the bureaucracy into what should have been secure employment.

Even as a child, he devalued anything his mother could understand. His father could read, his mother couldn't. Her 'little sayings' were the farthest extensions of her thought. They were also its everyday currency; how like the educated are the very, very foolish.

She would stand in the kitchen – another early memory – melting something over the gas. Keeler would watch, fascinated. It was a caramel-coloured, stubby candle, melting like a thick slab of frozen butter in its own battered saucepan. He liked the slow process of transformation, like blueing in the washtub, the tab of orange worked into the bowl of margarine, and this third thing, whatever it was.

But when it had finally melted, looking like burned butter, she smeared it over her face, wincing with the heat. When her face was entirely plastered in the stiffening caramel-coloured paste, and when it had hardened, she pulled it off. It hissed not only with heat but with the hundreds of hairs pulled off with it, and when it was all recollected, a twisted heap of cold beeswax back in the saucepan and wrapped in old aprons under the sink, his mother's face was pink and smooth and he was asked to feel it.

'Hot,' he said.

'Smooth?'

'A little.'

She sighed, made sure the pan was hidden. 'Ah well,' she said, 'don't let your father know.'

Keeler wanted to forget everything he'd seen.

'Let sleeping dogs lie,' she said.

The boy could picture them, fierce and mangy, sniffing out the saucepan under the sink, tearing open the aprons and wolfing down the cold wax with its old skin and stray black hairs. He came to associate her strange ritual with the yellow wax always with stray dogs; the lingering odour for years after was the odour of dogs and of some terrible unnatural operation that left his mother's cheeks hot and smooth.

Keeler's father was a carpenter by trade, but after hours and weekends he did other things: non-union work like plumbing and house painting and simple wiring. By day he was strictly a framer and roofer, and with the suburbs spreading all over the South Hills, there was construction enough to keep him busy.

He had all the skills to put up a house single-handedly if you weren't too choosy. He'd done it for other people, but the Keelers continued to rent. For Joe Keeler, owning a house was a dubious venture. New houses were always a little unfinished, and if he peeked into a wall or a window sash he would begin to price out the cost of repairs, calculate the builder's profit, and work himself into a rage. He was usually in a rage, and he hated builders. He hated the idea of anyone making a profit on his money. He even withheld what he considered an equitable amount of labour from any job. Renting, he practically got the duplex free after deducting for continual improvements. Renting or buying, his father told him, was six of one, half a dozen of another, and maybe because by then Keeler was seven or eight, he understood. His father was easier to understand anyway: Measure twice, cut once – that was Joe Keeler.

When he was ten, Keeler started going out on jobs with his father, nightly and weekends, carrying his tool kit or mitre box, holding ladders and spreading drop cloths. Keeler's father was lean; his pants always bunched around the belt loops as if there were clothespins holding them up. He had to keep a leather punch for adjusting his belts, always well beyond the last notch, and sometimes he had to cut off the unused part of the belt or else lap it back through the first two loops.

There were no subtleties in Keeler's life, no surprises. His father coughed like a dying man because he'd been secretly dying for a long time. In four years he would be dead, as anyone would have predicted, of lung cancer. The only time he'd gotten fat was a few weeks before the growth was detected. He'd had to let his belt out a notch to accommodate a painful little paunch just below his navel. 'Gettin' fat in my old age,' he'd said (he was forty-six), 'and sometimes it hurts like hell.'

His father enjoyed smoking more than any man Keeler had ever seen. He smoked with the total absorption of a wounded soldier on a stretcher whose cigarette is held for him by his buddy or medic. With every draw on the cigarette his breath shunted like a child's who'd been crying. On the rare moments that he took the cigarette from his lips, he would pinch it tightly to keep it from rolling, then set it on the nearest table edge. Every table and countertop featured charred parabolas, as regular as sawteeth, along the edges. The minute his father set down one cigarette, he absentmindedly lit another. That was the hardest thing coming home to after the funeral, all those black defacements. He smoked the butts right down to stubs that disappeared in the centre of his lips. When he extracted them he had to use two fingers, as though he were about to whistle for a taxi. All of this endowed smoking with a deep sense of ritual and mortality in the boy's mind; smoking was a calling, like carpentry, built on long apprenticeship and certification under fire. Keeler's grandfather, a drunken, arthritic old man who'd burned his toolbox rather than pass it down to Keeler's dad – the Keeler family was a study in a long career of spite – had perished in a smouldering easy chair, a smoker's death.

Keeler's father, younger and less careless, was to die a more protracted smoker's death. Keeler was fourteen when his father finally died. This earlier death, the one recorded here, happened two years earlier.

The apartment they were looking for was near the town centre of a suburb called Mount Lebanon. His father rarely ventured beyond downtown; Keeler himself had crossed over the bridges to the South Side only for annual trips to the county fair. This trip was to be by the Number 38 trolley to the end of the line. Whenever Keeler thought of Mount Lebanon, he thought of skies permanently blue and lawns as green as Forbes Field in June and of every house painted white and never flaking, as though they had been dipped in cream.

The village centre, where the trolley made its loop, was – on a wet, windy Saturday in March – as dark and dirty as any other place in the city. A theatre and an upholsterer's, shoe-repair shop and a grill, bakery and the tracks. Keeler and his father rode out on one of the old trolleys, the cane-seated, yellow ones that managed to look like raised and elongated roadsters, with their wide running boards, two saucer-like headlamps, and an elaborate wrought-iron cowcatcher in front. His father remembered as a boy watching these same trolleys tearing through the countryside, following the riverbeds and mountain flanks all the way east to Johnstown and downriver to Weirton and Wheeling. Riding a trolley to a different state struck Keeler as a kind of freedom he would never see; he had to be satisfied to be still able to ride one of the heroic old cars to Mount Lebanon. They were only in service on weekends and during rush hours, and they were to disappear completely, scrapped or sold to museums, in another year.

They walked downhill, Keeler holding his father's heavy box with both hands, and shifting the burden by a modified swinging from side to side. At the base of the street they found the building, an old five-storey apartment house with gilt numbers above the door and a name in gold leaf painted on the transom: ALHAMBRA. It was the sort of building with a long waiting list.

The inside walls were a cream-coloured stucco meringue. The wood trim was dark; the whole thing must have been put up in the Moorish period of the mid-twenties, when buildings were all named Babylon and Araby. There were real paintings in the common hallways and big chandeliers outside the stairwell on every floor, looking as out of place as the pictures he'd seen of chandeliers in the Moscow subway. No scrap papers, no empty bottles, no greasy paper sacks of undisposed garbage in the hall. This was Mount Lebanon. Their business was in apartment 5, third floor. Some plumbing, the woman had said. Then maybe some plastering and painting, if she liked the work.

The woman who answered the door didn't go with the old wood and stucco and watercolours in the hall. She was in her thirties, barely, with short black curls that fell over each other in layers, like skirts. She had one long set of eyelashes already attached and the other, like a smashed centipede, between her fingers. One set of shaped fingernails had been lacquered with the kind of red in the deepest crevice of a rose. Her eyes were black, velvety, but she wore no lipstick. Her cheeks were rough and blotchy. She was building herself from the rafters down, in defiance of sound carpentry principles. Below her eyes, everything but the nails was in a state of disrepair: a cluttered work site held together by a faded wrapper, like a tarp.

'About time,' she said. 'I see you brought a helper. Well, you're going to need all the help – just look.'

While Keeler's father paused to light a cigarette, Keeler took in the sights. First, the shallow tubs out on the kitchen floor, the mop propped against the sink, and a puddle of alarming dimensions. But far more wondrous to Keeler was the sight of the half-formed lady, from the pink slippers up: her ankles were chapped and veined, her shins shiny except for small nicks and scrapes – shining the way his mother's cheeks and chin would shine after the layers of wax. Perhaps some women bathed in wax and came out looking like apples. Lugging the box, he followed his father to the kitchen. She said from just behind him, 'This gave out this morning.'

A fine spray shot out from under the sink. Even Keeler knew that a twist on the main shut-off valve was all that it needed. His father pinched the cigarette and balanced it on her countertop. Then he reached under the sink and stopped the water.

'Better get this mopped up right away,' he told the woman. 'If your linoleum has leaks, it'll seep right through.'

'I'm busy,' she said.

'Frankie –'

The woman walked out through the dining room, which was enclosed by heavy doors with leaded glass panels, then down a corridor to her bedroom. Keeler wrung the mop by hand and started in at the puddle's shoreline, pushing it out toward the walls, then spreading the deeper parts back over it. A process like painting in reverse: every coat thinner, tending to a final disappearance.

The first time he saw her, it was accidental. The bathroom was in his line of vision at the very end of the corridor. When he looked up from his mopping, she was leaning over the sink to hook on a brassiere. It was all over in a split second, but Keeler replayed it, stunned, for several minutes. By then she'd put her wrapper back on. His father was sawing through a rusty pipe.

Just in time, Keeler spotted the old cigarette, beginning to smoulder. Her countertop was plastic and the burn was very light yellow. He rubbed it out.

She stood by her lavatory in the same pink slippers and bathrobe, leaning forward to inspect her face. He could sense somehow that she'd forgotten all about the men in her kitchen.

God, if he hadn't been mopping! If he'd just looked up ten seconds earlier and seen the whole thing! He'd never forgive himself, seeing his first naked lady, and it being in Mount Lebanon. Right now she was safely under wraps, but anything could happen.

She turned on her taps; the pipes coughed. His father from under the sink grunted, 'Damn fool.' From far down the hall, the lady turned. Keeler applied himself quickly to unnecessary mopping. She was on her way to the kitchen now, eating up the space between them.

The transformation had spread to her second eye and both cheeks. It was as though her eyes were speaking, as if the top half of her face were two feet closer and ten years younger than the rest of her. Her eyes were soft, loving, densely lashed. It was as though only part of her were in focus.

Her voice, as he expected, was cruel and shallow. 'Can't you see that I'm trying to get ready … to go out?' She was standing over his father where his legs issued from under the sink. From down below came the magnified exertions of his father, coughing with a smoker's snarl; even his normal breathing was like a lion's purr. He held a section of an S-trap in his hand and he swirled his fingers in it, extracting grease and hairs, entwined like brick.

'Well, what do you propose to do?'

He offered her a glimpse of his finger, wedged in the pencil-thin opening. The he reached up and placed the section of pipe on her counter. She didn't look.

There was no mistaking that she was getting ready to go out and that she expected all the help that electricity and plumbing could give. Keeler had never seen his father on his knees in front of anyone, especially not an angry woman, and the effect was exciting. It made Keeler look at the woman from the floor up, undoing her decoration, and it made him respond to the perverse intimacy of all the layers of her dowdy clothes, so at odds with the top six inches of her face. It made him think of flesh, alien textures, and the way flesh must feel in the richer suburbs of Pittsburgh, so different from his mother's hot waxy stubble. And his father stood up, very slowly, lifting the cigarette out with two clamped fingers, letting his eyes drift upward, insolently, as he stood.

She didn't like that. Keeler felt, at that moment, that if he had not been there, his father would have attacked the woman. Or she would have clawed him and screamed. And in all his life, he'd never seen his father turn his head at a woman, whistle, stare, or even tell a dirty story.

'Please, just leave,' she said.

'Then you won't get nobody to fix that there pipe.'

'I really don't care. I have ten minutes before my fiancé comes, and I want you out.'

He flipped over the sides of his tool kit with his boot, and Keeler sealed it. Then he ground out the butt.

'Suit yourself. When in Rome.'

'What do I owe you?'

'I dint do nothin'.'

'If you'd been on time, you would have finished.'

'I don't make appointments, lady. You still got an hour's work there. That piece was totally froze out. I gotta cut a new section and solder it in.'

'Come back tomorrow then. I'll be in at two o'clock.' She said this like a big concession. Tomorrow was Sunday, and Keeler's father had never gotten up before two o'clock on a Sunday except to catch a Steelers game on television. He never finished dressing on Sunday; some days a shirt but no pants, other days the opposite. It was March, between all sports seasons.

'Too busy tomorrow. Come on, Frankie.'

'Here.' She held out money, two coins. 'For the boy at least. He did the mopping.'

His father didn't stop him from accepting the fifty cents.

Yes, definitely, the woman had affected them both. A woman couldn't show a man into her apartment, dressed like that and adopting such an attitude (while being already half-beautiful and giving promise of completing the job) without becoming for Keeler the prototype of all beautiful women. For his father, the most perfect bitch. Together, father and son, they were consumed by lust. One beginning to die, the other too young. And they left.

Down the stuccoed halls, with Keeler carrying the tools, they lumbered, down the staircase like an elephant with bells on. When they got to the first floor, a short Italian man with shoulder pads of hair lifting up his undershirt squinted up at Keeler's father and asked, 'Plumber?'

By way of an answer, his father lifted his hand in the general direction of the street. It was his ambition to own a panel truck some day: JOE KEELER GENERAL CONTRACTING, it would say. For an instant, as his father pointed, Keeler could see that truck parked out front. Light blue, it would be. Something self-explanatory for nosy janitors.

'What makesa you t'ink, hah, you can come inna the front, hah? There'sa the back for pipple like you.'

From inside the super's apartment the opened door revealed two young men as thick as their father, only taller and blonder, with wives, children, mothers and grandmothers, and a tricycle being pedalled around a dining table. The Keelers followed his pointing finger down to the basement and up through a bulkhead that opened on the back alley. The flesh on Keeler's fingertips was beginning to split.

They were walking now, back to the trolley loop. It had turned dark, with bits of freezing rain stinging their faces. His father growled behind him, coughing and spitting.

'Fixed her good, huh? She won't have a drop of water till Monday. If then.'

Keeler was working on one of his agonized generalizations: the whole exercise had seemed to him a demonstration of some great truth about pride and discomfort and, in his father's case, laziness. Now she wouldn't have water, and his father would miss out on least ten dollars. And he would miss seeing her again, in her Sunday clothes. 'That sure teaches her to act smart with me, huh? Cut off her nose is what she done.' He seemed to be laughing, but laughter – with those two gluey pits he called lungs – ended up half killing him every time. Nose, nose? Keeler had heard something about cutting off one's nose to do something equally stupid, but it wouldn't come to him. Nothing would come to him. His father stopped, bent double in the classic posture of a man being sick, but it was the cough, first lowering him, then bobbing his head like punches. Keeler rested the toolbox.

He stood a few feet above his father. Ahead of him lay the trolley tracks. None of the old trolleys was waiting, but one of the sleek new ones, with silent, effective fans in the summer and a row of solitary window seats up front, had just turned off Washington Road onto the loop. And below him he could still see Alhambra, where they'd been forced to exit through the basement by the garbage cans. There'd been a hand-painted sign over the bulkhead: TRADESMEN AND LABORERS. The sign was wondrous to him, a definition of himself he'd never considered.

His father stopped coughing once they boarded the trolley. He took a window seat and fell asleep as the trolley started moving. When he couldn't smoke, he usually slept. Keeler had the whole car, the long corridor up to the driver, practically to himself. Somewhere on that trip a kind of fire rose up in him, and he said in a voice so loud it surprised him, 'I'm going to do things with my life. No one is ever going to tell me where to go. No one but me is going to tell me what to do, ever.'

The Unwanted Attention
of Strangers

In 1954, I was fourteen years old, an awkward, introverted boy imprisoned in my parents' suburban Pittsburgh furniture store. I spent my summer days and winter weekends at the store, avoiding my father and helping with the deliveries and uncrating, handling the bank deposits and bringing back coffee and food from the nearest short order counter. My father left the running of the store to my mother, who handled sales and bookkeeping. She in turn supervised our refugee refinisher, Ted Zablonsky, who worked in the back room restoring woods that came in damaged. Everything in retail furniture arrives nicked or splintered; Ted was the soul of the operation. There was a driver, Troy, for lifting and delivering, with my assistance.

My father put in the occasional appearance that summer, usually on weekends, while my mother rested and shopped, but he was officially 'scouting properties' for a larger store he intended to build in the hills near the Greater Pittsburgh airport. That was his cover. Sometimes he'd drop me at the airport for the day. I could spend eight hours strolling from gate to gate just staring at people who'd arrived from Los Angeles or were going to New York. Sometimes I'd pretend I was the traveller, bound for Tampa or Phoenix. I ached at the thought of any travel, but especially Europe. I'd memorized the grids of New York and traced out *Dragnet* shows on a roadmap of Los Angeles. Europe, where I had a small claim, was the only place left. I thought of the airport as being close to foreignness as Pittsburgh ever got.

He didn't pull in much before dawn most mornings. My mother, who rarely slept, would be sipping tea in the kitchen. He'd go straight to bed and sleep till three, then dress up to meet his lady friend for drinks at a roadhouse and dinner in a downtown restaurant. Sometimes, driven by the need for an alibi, or perhaps even an abiding interest in appearing innocent (he combined spontaneous deception with suicidal guilelessness), he would have his lady friend pick him up at our house in her grey Coupe de Ville. She'd done well in previous divorces. I'd have to join them for an hour of property-gazing.

Their painful bad acting and feigned interest in my opinion were humiliating to me. Her name was Mary, spelled with a final 'i' like a cross between Mata and Hari, according to my mother. She was in her thirties, an ash blonde with a full bosom and layers of make-up and a broad Pittsburgh accent that sounded half-cockney. She truly was a real estate agent, though she looked and acted like any hard blond actress whose roles called on her to break up marriages and drive older men crazy. At fourteen, I was slow to understand the meaning of passion, and thoroughly naive about evil and corruption, but it was a magic year and everything was on the verge of clarification.

Our store occupied a building that had filled the pockets of many investors over its eighty years. Now suburban and rustic with a wide gravelled parking lot around it, it had been built to resemble a Transylvanian hunting lodge. In those years, it stood deep in the woods, three hours from a post–Civil War Pittsburgh along a country trail. When big game fled to the nearby hills in the wake of trolley tracks and a two-lane highway, it was converted to a country inn and restaurant, but always one with a shady reputation.

During Prohibition it had prospered as a booze depot. In the thirties it added false panels to block off a room of gaming tables. Troy, our driver who'd grown up in the area, showed me the hidden alarm buzzers under the floorboards by the front door. During the war, the back rooms had been turned over to B-girls. Just before we rented it, it had been a teenage hangout where fast girls and hot cars congregated, and booze was routinely served to minors. When six drunk teenage regulars were killed in an accident, the restaurant was closed, the town's bribed policemen were put on trial, and the 'Olde Lodge' was all but gutted by a mob that stormed it like extras on the set of Castle Frankenstein. We got it cheap and put all our energy and all the money we could borrow into it. We converted the back rooms into a receiving area and repair shop, Ted's place. We took it out of its long inheritance of illicit pleasures and into the domesticated world of furniture.

Ted and my mother each worked to background music. Their separate radios were set to a classical station that I could never find when I spun the dial alone at night. At the store, between errands and deliveries, I would sit on a distant sofa and draw designs of everything around me: furniture, appliances, cars, buses, planes, skyscrapers. I had pretensions that had manifested themselves as talents: music and art and even some science. It was mimicry only. I could observe and imitate enough to please my mother, which was all I really cared about.

She had just turned fifty. In the previous year she'd had a hysterectomy, and the first of many small operations for skin cancer. She cushioned the affected area, the glasses-pit on the side of her nose, with dabs of gauze or tissue paper. In a couple of years, her marriage of nearly twenty years would be over. In the end, the furniture would all be auctioned off and I would be living with her in a dingy suburban town called, misleadingly, Castle Shannon, sleeping on a rollaway bed in her kitchen. My pretensions to a special place in the universe would fade. Membership in everything that Pittsburgh offers its selected youth, the Art Students' League, the Young Astronomers, the Junior Archaeologists and the Allegheny Country Junior Symphony, would lapse.

In that special year before the immanent became manifest, I liked to watch Ted perform his magic. His real name was Tadeusz, which he pronounced like a slushy Thaddeus. He was fifty-seven, but for all he'd lived through, the Nazis and the Russians, displacement to South Africa and Canada and finally to Pittsburgh, he could have been a hundred. He thought in global terms. He called it a fallen planet, a cursed century.

He didn't mind talking to me about Europe. I was an avid Europhile, especially the Europe of his childhood before the First World War. Even provincial Polish life shared the ideals of high bourgeois culture. He'd had violin training at the Lodz Conservatory, his older sisters were all pianists. His Italian mother had Venetian relatives. His banker father had owned a cottage on the Baltic, and their summers were an endless trek of spas and regal hotels between Lithuania and Venice.

Unfortunately I was a child of the Cold War and the still-glowing embers of McCarthyism. Poland had been banished from my sterilized vision of Europe, along with Czechoslovakia and the Balkans. Pittsburgh's Poles were Steeler fans, coarse as pig-iron and nearly as dense. Europe for me was France and Germany, and Italy in a pinch. Its ongoing reality had ceased after my mother's student years in Germany and her escape just twenty years before.

Twenty years didn't seem that long to me. I had a stamp album that stopped with the 1940 issues – the year of my birth – and 1940 seemed to be fresh, a cosmic yesterday. But her Europe and Ted's was an eon back.

Ted embodied the old culture and the mortal decline. Every gesture was slow and authoritative; he laid out his tools like a surgeon, he surveyed damage like a golfer lining up his putt. He rolled out his day's cigarettes first thing in the morning, spacing them at intervals around each job. And he liked us. When my mother or I said, 'Ted', he'd raise his head and smile. 'Madame', he'd say, or elaborately, 'Young master'. If Troy or my father said it, he responded with a silent brace of his shoulders, a cock of the ear.

He combed his full head of hair straight back without a part. Very European, I thought. His American wife, Bella, did the cutting. They had a farm twenty miles north of Pittsburgh; Bella baked and the three sons – blond, crew-cut boys, compact and powerfully built, all born here – raised pigs and fruit trees. They pickled and preserved and cultivated a vegetable garden. Leftovers they sold. They were a self-sufficient little community waiting for the next apocalypse.

He was not without his vanities. He was accustomed to being watched and admired. He dyed his hair with glints of brown and cordovan, blended with a strand or two of black, some of red, with the same feel for highlight and nuance that he brought to wood. It looked like streaks of polished mahogany, or the honeyed maple of my cello. When he unfolded his small, round, wire-rimmed glasses from their blue velvet case with its Warszawa address still clearly stamped, I felt it as an *occasion*. I could hear a Milton Cross voice in the background, 'Now Maestro Zablonsky puts on his glasses, he selects a cigarette, he snaps the case shut and returns it to his pocket, striking a match across the roughened skin on the palm of his hand and the match ignites, filling the room with a fragrance unlike anything in American smoking…'

He'd had a wife and a much larger family in Poland, now lost to him. One son had survived. That boy was thirty-five, married, living in London and not in communication.

The most remarkable feature of Ted was his hands. A furniture refinisher works with knives and an imitation forest of hardened fillers, to be melted and mixed and worked with a painter's eye into the gouges and nicks. He needs a burner for melting the sticks and blades for working the molten drops, buffers and sanders, clamps and glues to make the repairs invisible.

Over the years, the hands make effective substitutes: he stropped the blades against the grey raised calluses on the flat of his hand. He drew blood from the backs of his fingers, sometimes in a test of sharpness, other times to work bloodstains into the wood. He tested the heat of his putty knife against the tip of his little finger and worked the molten material into the wood as though it were nothing warmer than tallow drippings from a restaurant Chianti bottle. Finer than the finest sandpaper were his blunt, roughened fingertips, each of them missing one or two joints. All of it, he claimed, was painless, but his threshold must not have registered in human terms. Sometimes he would pinch strips of bonded wood together between his thumb and two thick stumps of finger, and excess glue would spurt from the joints as though under the pressure of several tons.

Many years later, sometime in my late twenties, I was confronting questions of my own survival. I was married, trying to be the young writer living in Europe. From our balcony on the rue des Écoles, we could watch Paris burning.

With my old copy of Céline's *Death on the Installment Plan* in hand, we'd tramped through the dingy stalls of the old *passages* areas he'd written about. Feeling literary, we'd looked for a café, only to confront a mob of students passing out broadsheets, peddlers running through the streets pursued by charging policemen. At streetcorners, cars were burning and knots of students had clustered at the top of the Métro stairs chanting, '*Lisez, demandez, l'Humanité!*'

In a matter of hours, Paris had closed down. Taxi-drivers struck cardboard signs in their windows, *Frontière belge, 500 frs.* We walked back to our hotel through the middle of the riots, moneyless, foodless. Those next few weeks were the last stop in the long disenchantment. Europe no longer fulfilled an ancient fantasy. I thought again of that older Europe, the high-bourgeois ideal that these students were attacking, and somewhere in those weeks of scrounging for food at black market prices, becoming rats of Paris on the Céline model, reading the student broadsheets and the official responses of the *Patronat,* I felt the truth of Ted Zablonsky's old lesson: Europe was a dead whore crawling with maggots. I went back to reading Thomas Mann. And suddenly I knew who Ted Zablonsky was. More to the point, I knew who Ted had been and what he represented.

I thought of his hands, Conservatory hands, long fingers softened in oil, lost to frostbite in Lithuania. I saw his wanting to die, cursing his absurd survival in a Pittsburgh furniture store, and I began crying for that, because he never knew he could never die.

He was Tadzio, one of the immortals.

And so Ted and my mother, when there were no customers, would sit in the back as he worked, or as she sipped tea made on her hotplate, and listen to music and talk of his children or of furniture, and of Europe. They were a strange couple, she with the dab of gauze under her glasses, he with the slabs of dead skin, grey and heavy as coats of concrete encrusting his hands, and his long, reddish hair that flopped down on his forehead in thin, delicate crescents. He attacked his work from a pianist's posture with the minute concentration on a lap-high task that bent his back and curved his neck.

'We had some Polish students in my school,' my mother might be saying. 'I always thought them exceptionally brave and cultured. They came from the best families, and spoke French to the professors, even the ones we knew were Nazi.'

Ted would pause, then stare at her over the tops of his wire-rim glasses. 'I would say those teachers took their revenge.'

She would try to remember the names of the students, back nearly twenty-five years to the other universe she'd come from. It was the world that excluded me, yet over which I had genetic claim, and the confusion excited me. Europe was like a distant relative who'd died, leaving me estates.

'I was in Germany when you were there, and France and Italy,' Ted said one day. 'Perhaps we passed each other on the street. Did you go to concerts? Perhaps you heard me play, but have forgotten me.' He reached for his wallet, picking it deftly with those stubby fingers, and flipped it open. Even the wallet was hand-stitched, tanned from pigs raised on his farm. 'Take it out,' he said.

It was an old newspaper photo of Ted in his youth with his name in Italian, I presumed, underneath it. It was a formal studio portrait, the artist in tuxedo, reminiscent of a young Gary Cooper or any number of

Hollywood stars, hair and ears fashionably unfocused in the twenties manner, but with eyes and mouth so alive that I half expected sympathetic static on our radio, like those sputters in movie soundtracks for every electric sparkle on the screen. His hair was perfectly blond, and just as full and precisely combed as it was that day in Pittsburgh. He was smiling again, through rotten teeth. He knew the effect his picture would have. One either fell in love with it, or cried at the remnant he'd become.

My mother only whispered, 'My God.' It meant, *No, I would not forget this.*

I was embarrassed for her, then for him. 'Is that your real name?' I asked, trying to read the caption. 'Tadzio?'

'Italians, they call me that, my mother, my cousins. My father called me Tadziu.'

'How old are you here?' she asked.

'This is early picture. My manager, he told me, you are golden-haired, we start you in Italy. If you are black-haired, we start you in Sweden. It was all the same. Europe was all the same. Here, I am twenty-four only. It is 1921, in Milano. You see, *Corriere della Sera.*'

My mother was busy figuring. She would have been twenty, a school-girl outside Leipzig. It was the time of the riots and the Inflation. Thousands, millions, of marks for a loaf of bread. She'd read me stories. She'd had to postpone college and so had worked in a fabric store and begun designing clothing. Later, she designed furniture fabrics, then chairs and sofas and tables and that took her to an *atelier* of the Bauhaus. We had the books at home, which I had dutifully memorized. It didn't matter she said, none of it mattered. She had lived the life of her century. It didn't matter if she saw nothing else. She didn't expect anything more. How much are we privileged to know? She had seen her tables and lamps on exhibition, she'd seen her name, assumed to have died in the war, in post-war catalogues. She had known the Masters. All that, and she'd been spared and she'd had a child with all her gifts, and more. This was the story she told, this was the life I was destined to surpass. And now this ancient newspaper photo of her current employee leaped out at her like a missing link between two worlds.

I suddenly wanted to know, and so I asked. 'Ted, why did you quit?'

It was a gauche question; artists don't quit, they abandon their works, or their lives. He could have shown me his stumps of fingers, but that would have been sophistry. He'd quit before the war. He took a puff on his cigarette. His teeth were bad, rotting as we spoke. 'I was just tired,' he said. 'You stop to take a rest, and suddenly you are no more.'

'Tired of what?'

'Young master, I think tired most from the attentions of strangers.'

'Are you sorry you quit?'

'Many times sorry. They asked me, come to America long, long time ago, and play. I did not know my power, I was young and from a backward place. I could come to America and play for the movies and be rich or keep touring Europe and be famous. Everyone was going to America so maybe it was a good time to stay in Europe, yes? But I tell you honest, I didn't think of money or of fame. I didn't think, If I go to America I miss the war, I miss … this … I save my family. I was in love with a married lady and her husband would not move to America for her, that's the only truth. So I stayed. I hope I'm not shocking you, madame, it's just a silly story.'

'But very European,' said my mother.

Her stories of Europe had made me feel I belonged there. Every boy my age was sawing on his cello, playing soccer, digging up Roman pottery, designing and sketching. Without Hitler, I'd have been such a child. But older and maybe dead or East German. All that was noble in her life, worthy of study and even of imitation, came from Europe. About the other Europe, the one that had let her down, she was too embarrassed to speak. After 1933 there was a blank in her life, most of it occupied by marriage and motherhood and moves across the face of America. Marriage was her surrender to nihilism.

So Europe for both of them was a golden moment, toasting them with glory, but at a horrible price. Ted had lost a family and a country and a career and a language. He'd joined the Polish resistance, flown out of Britain, crashed, lost his fingers, been captured. He survived the Nazis, but he and his fellow officers were rounded up by the Russians. At a mass execution against a pit they'd had to dig themselves, he was saved, he said, by a shower of blood. Bodies fell on top of him, keeping him warm until the Russians walked away. Many of my father's friends and most of the travelling salesmen who stopped by the store had 'war stories', but most of them were prefaced with a request that my mother and I had better leave the room. They could go all night with their stories, and often did. Ted didn't talk much, but didn't mind who heard him. Europe he called a dead whore; the Germans, the Russians, the Poles in exile or in power – all dead whores, or maggots feasting on the corpse.

I didn't believe it. I needed the concept of Europe, a place still untouched by crime and vulgarity, by commerce, by the struggles my father had with Teamster delivery men who deliberately dropped furniture if we weren't ready with a 'detrucking fee' when they knocked on the door, by Mafia neon workers and Mafia garbage-haulers who stood around the office waiting for their 'insurance', by customers who refused to pay, by the fake prices I penned on tags in order to cross them out with a lower fake price, by the hours of his profane threats on the telephone to factories, to deliverers, to salesmen about promises made and broken – by the whole sad business of doing business in America. All that, and its external quintessence, Mari. Between that America, which I knew too well, and the Europe of artistic marvels, to which I also ascribed integrity and cleanliness and a decent respect for the marital vows, I knew which to choose. Ted's stories, like my mothers, were still more attractive than anything I knew in Pittsburgh.

One day, Troy offered me escape of a different sort. He was willing to sacrifice an hour of his free time after work, he said, for a special delivery. For this, he'd need to borrow my mother's car, not the truck. I got him the keys.

I recognized the route almost immediately. On to the expressway, through the tunnels and out towards the airport. Our delivery was in a small grocery sack and I peeked in, expecting bed parts or dresser handles. What we were delivering was a five-pound bag of brown sugar.

'I just found out that bitch's address,' said Troy, handling my mother's Rambler like a roadster. He was six foot seven, and had to cradle the steering wheel between his knees. 'Oooo-ee, is that baby gonna smell!'

On the way out he told me his grievance. He'd been sent to Mari's by my father to clean out her basement and do some kitchen painting. To my father, Troy was a hired man whose time belonged to the store for any purpose. Troy had been an All-State basketballer. He was still remembered in the area, he was far more famous than Ted or my mother. He'd lost out on college because of the war, but the war had made him a professional infantry driver. He'd seen his own Europe. He'd driven in Korea and Japan. He'd driven from Frankfurt down to Salerno. He'd driven on the left in England. He knew European women, oh my, yes. My mother's respect for Troy's professionalism, along with Ted's refusal to lift or strain and my frequent absences for school, had forced her to push and carry furniture alone and led to the hernia that preceded the hysterectomy. Everything, I learned that summer, is connected. Every life, no matter how anonymous, touches on the great events of the century. If a boy can't leave Pittsburgh for Europe, Europe will come to the boy in Pittsburgh.

By the time we got to Mari's split-level house in Greentree, I had an idea of what sugar could do to a Cadillac engine. I also had my marching orders: a giant black man on a street in Greentree would cause an immediate panic. He would wait for me around the corner. I was to sneak past the driveway, check out the house, and, with the funnel that Troy had lifted from Ted's workbench, would empty a pound of Jamaica Brown down the gullet of a Coupe de Ville.

'She done stole your daddy!' is how Troy put it. 'She's making your mama crazy.' And later, 'She's just a baa-ad woman, man. She deserves anything we give her. She's *lucky* it's only sugar in her fuel line.' It didn't take much to convince me. I was off on the adventure of my life, the only conscious evil I'd ever committed in fourteen exemplary years. I'd often wondered about the world's moral balance, and now I was about to test it. People like me and my mother who never asked for favours, never took even their proper share, who apologized for giving orders or showing the slightest temper – didn't we balance out people like my father, and Troy, whose outrageous exploits and petty crimes were the conversational bedrock of our daily deliveries?

Both cars, my father's blue and white Riviera and Mari's grey Coupe de Ville, were in the driveway. I'd drawn that Buick a hundred times; this was the year of GM's big design breakthrough, and showrooms had been packed. My father and I had gone from Impala to Olds 88s right up to Riviera because we couldn't believe the wraparound windows and the sporty little hump over the back wheelhouse and those new two-tone colour schemes. Nineteen fifty-four was a magic year. Maybe it was

Buick design and my father's sense of sudden empowerment that led to Mari and not vice versa.

I stopped at a hedge next to the driveway. 'Hodges' said the mailbox. Mari Hodges. Who would guess the secrets of such a name? The living room drapes were drawn. The cars were so long my father's Buick nearly touched the sidewalk. The quiet little crescent of split-level homes was nearly deserted. Houses were distinguished by different paint jobs and different window panels in the front doors.

I casually brushed against the Buick's gas tank. It was locked. Of course, my father had taken that option, the internal tank release, to guard against cases of almost classic vengeance. I peered at the sides of the Cadillac and found no little door at all. Never having owned a Cadillac, I knew nothing about pulling back the licence plate.

There came a click, not loud, but sharp enough to shock me. It came from the garage door release, and by the time I reached the hedge, the door was clattering open and I heard a voice, my father's, the sound of a falling tree in a forest that I should not have heard, calling back, 'All aboooard! This choo-choo is sidewalk bound!' He paused at the open door to light a cigarette. Never be seen in public without a cigarette. 'Sure there's nothing more? Last chance!' The voice and appearance was my father's. But never had I heard such words, such lightness from him.

My father and a garbage can, a sight never before seen on this planet, rolling it on its side and conducting it along the driveway on the far side of the parked cars, out to the curb. Never in his married life had my father carried garbage. Never had he cooked a meal, washed a dish, or done laundry. He was a short, well-dressed grey-haired man singing to himself as he set the garbage can straight and jiggled it a few times in order to fit the lid on tight. I had never seen him when he wasn't aware of being watched, by me, my mother, or a customer. I didn't know how to process the image, it was like the nude pictures of women that Troy showed me on deliveries. They temporarily decomposed the world around me.

'Yeah, did it,' I said when I ran back to the Rambler, throwing the funnel in first. Troy slapped the steering wheel and emitted his long, high squeal of delight, 'Yeh-yuh! The whole one pound? Oh, man, I want to be here!' But we were gone in an instant.

* * *

I didn't want to know how bad things had gotten. Because my father hadn't seen me that evening, I believed I hadn't seen him. The same man couldn't be so different – a little silly, helpful and friendly – compared with what I saw at home. Taking the garbage out was the most serious thing a man like my father could do. And catching him at it, singing, calling the garbage can a choo-choo was worse somehow than catching those little signs between them in the car. It made me inexpressibly sad, a low cello note, and left me with none of my protective hate.

One morning when I was still asleep in the basement game room, my mother burst into the room holding an icepack to her nose. Her eye was already black, blood had caked on her split upper lip. 'Can I go into the store like this?' she was asking, and I demanded, 'Did *he* do this?' but she denied it, saying only she'd walked into the door in the dark.

And there were the times I saw her in the office with her head collapsed on the desk in the nest of her arms, like a child in study-hall, and I'd be afraid to disturb her not because she was sleeping but because her shoulders were shaking. I would head off customers in the front, and try to serve them, though inwardly I died meeting anyone.

She grew more and more dependent on Ted. Customers would storm into the back room when I had failed to intercept them or when I was back there myself, demanding, 'Well, what does a person have to do around here to get served?' Ted never said anything improper, never offered a judgement about my father or Mata Hari. He'd become a silent confessor or perhaps an analyst, and sometimes on their lunch hours my mother would pour them wine or, as he preferred, a beer. I felt I was losing her, sometimes to German, sometimes merely to a wistful silence they both enjoyed, along with the classical music.

That was the summer I would sit out front over a black Formica cocktail table and put my drawings aside in order to muss up my hair and watch the dandruff pour down, like dingy stars in a Pittsburgh sky, and I started noticing the hair I was losing, at not yet fifteen. I could make a ball of hairs and dandruff; this ball of deadness is me, I remember thinking. It was all so desperately sad, my mother's gauze on the nose, my father rolling out a garbage can. I had never known beauty, never even drawn it or played it, all I did so well was the sheerest imitation and I hated my cello and my drawings. I was becoming a freak rather than getting older and closer to the answers.

My mother would reach for Ted's hands; I saw that when I wasn't supposed to. He didn't pull away. She pulled them closer, held then to her cheek, seemed to kiss them. He stared at her. Once, I saw, he brought his other hand to her cheek and she ran back to the office.

I met Bella that summer. She started by driving Ted to work at eight o'clock, then taking the car – she'd gotten a job, teaching music part-time in a local school – and picking him up at four. She was short and chubby, with dark hair cut in bangs and gathered in a school-girl ponytail. Ted was in the habit of opening up the back every morning – we didn't officially open till ten – so my mother didn't meet Bella until the first or second afternoon of the new arrangement.

She was always good at meeting people, anyone, no matter how she felt inside. I think she wanted to like Bella, or was prepared to like her, but Bella was of this time and place, Pittsburgh in the fifties. Ted and my mother weren't. She knew herself and she knew what she wanted, and they didn't.

I ran to the back when I heard the shouting. The three of them were clustered by the door. 'Keep your dirty hands off Tadzio, you dirty, dirty, woman,' Bella was screaming, and my mother's face was a frozen smile of incredulity. She raised her hands, palms open in explanation, but words wouldn't come.

'We go,' said Ted. 'Come,' with a smile to my mother, and a heavy hand on Bella's sleeve.

'Madame, I assure you –' and now my mother took three or four running half steps towards the door, to embrace the woman, I think, but Bella spilled out the door and nearly sprawled onto the gravel parking lot.

'Dirty, dirty, shame on you,' came the call from down below our loading dock as my mother and I stood on the delivery steps and Ted clawed for the keys to open the door.

'Shame!' she was still crying. 'Shame, shame!'

Identity

Porter, Reg and Hennie. My parents for several years. Mysteries to me, to each other. Gone now, even in name.

My earliest memory is of falling off an armchair when I was three and breaking my arm. A bad break, poorly mended. Even now the extended arm, with the elbow resting, barely grazes the tabletop. For the wrist and hand to conspire with gravity is an act of will. Think of the forearm as I do, a slow hypotenuse connecting that original fracture to a slightly skewed grand disclosure. Needless to say, I'm still waiting for it.

I'd been watching my father reading and writing in a Queen Anne chair. For years that memory stood as evidence that we'd been a normal, happy family. Father reading, son at his side, a little spill, nothing too serious. Despite the small imperfection it left me, it is a pleasant memory. It occurred to me since, however, that we never owned Queen Anne furniture, especially not in 1943, and that I cannot remember my father ever reading or writing. When I was thirteen and having to learn to read and write all over again, I discovered something else I'd always suspected: my father couldn't read or write at all.

That same year, 1943, I remember sitting on my tricycle at the top of a steep hill. This part of the memory is a moment, even now, of rather intense pleasure. And then I flung my legs out straight and rode like the breeze to the bottom of the little hill. Unfortunately, the hill was our driveway and the bottom of it was our garage door, and the door was down. From that episode, I received a bent nose, a broken collarbone and a skull fracture. After the fracture I became an epileptic. It was bad as a child, not so severe now. From internal evidence, you will conclude that I'm writing this as a man of forty-three.

Such are the sheltering memories of childhood. Or the preferred fictions of adulthood. I once overheard my mother, talking to a friend long after I'd grown up, relate a more intriguing version of those same injuries. There'd never been a chair or a tricycle and garage door. There'd only been New Year's Eve, 1943, and a scrounged-up baby-sitter recommended by someone down at Sears, where my father worked. And she had a soldier husband who'd wangled a holiday pass, only to find her apartment empty. He saw our address on a piece of paper. He confronted her there, in our second-floor apartment on Reading Road, stabbed her and shot her visiting boyfriend, and then went to work on me, his only witness. So I was killed, at least to his satisfaction. I have never, consciously, been able to replay a single frame of that incident. So much for the theories of Freud or the plots of Ross Macdonald. I think of the armchair and the tricycle constantly.

Let more bones break, more moves be made. Those early memories are from Cincinnati –a freak appearance in our lives, a town that did not claim us – from deep in America, a country, as it turned out, that did not claim me either.

Turned out, not in the passive sense of a plot that runs its course, but in the active sense of total reversal, like a pocket being turned out, like deadbeats being turned out of a bar. There are millions like me on this continent (I know, I meet them everywhere) who constitute no bloc, and who, for all their numbers, have no champion. The implications radiate like angles from a protractor, like tracks from a roundhouse, though I'm unable to pursue them all. Think rather of Reg and Hennie Porter and me, lying just a degree or two off plumb, or the prime horizontal axis. Think of life led slightly off balance.

In Pittsburgh in 1952 I was standing on the roof of an apartment building, with matches, a knife and rabbit ears under opaque plastic. With matches I burned off an inch or so, stripped it with the knife, then spliced the copper onto the frail set of rabbit ears that had come with our first television set. Then I lashed the whole contraption to the giant brick apartment-house chimney and crawled to the edge of the roof and called down, 'How about it now?'

Staring down six floors to our opened window on the second floor was the closest thing I knew to an epileptic aura. The sidewalk yo-yoed, close enough to step out on.

Peter Humphries, my only friend, was in our apartment. He was from the third floor. My parents both worked, so did his mother. His father did not seem to exist, even in memory.

He shouted up, 'It's just a test pattern!'

He couldn't know that that was the whole point. I'd succeeded. It meant to me – though it was only channel 9 in Steubenville, Ohio, or 7 in Wheeling, West Virginia – that features were materializing from outer space. New test patterns, new readers of local news, new advertisers, new street names, different phrasing of the same Tri-State weather, different politics: the mark of sophistication was access to all the channels. I'd exhausted KDKA, and the only NBC outlet before we got our own WIIC on channel 11 was channel 6 in Johnstown. Farther out in the mountains there was rumoured to be a channel 10 in Altoona and a channel 3 downriver in Huntington, West Virginia. Pittsburgh, in other words, was an exciting place, if you had the right connections. Pittsburgh eventually got more than enough channels, but not in 1952. We were always deprived, last in everything, at least in the years I lived there. But with ingenuity and agility and rabbit ears lashed to a chimney, hope existed for more than snow on channels 2, 3, 6, 7, 9 and 13, which was educational. On exceptional nights with my antenna pointing in the right direction I'd gotten Cleveland, and Chambersburg, almost in Maryland. A collector with luck could get a picture, however furry, and enough voice to make a positive identification, on every VHF channel, and he could pull in signals from four states, not counting freaks, which once, with the help of clouds, sunspots and a low-flying airplane, brought in Detroit and Buffalo.

The point is, I was king of the airwaves. I might not have known much about my parents or myself, or about Peter Humphries for that matter, but those questions never arose. I knew the important things, like call letters and the names of news readers and where to shop for Mercurys and Fords in Steubenville. It was the essence of my new-found teenagerliness to know everything about strangers and occult signals materializing from snow, and to know nothing at all about the forces that had made me, the scars and handicaps that were about to reclaim me.

All of this happened nearly thirty year ago. I haven't seen Pittsburgh in a quarter of a century, and probably all those familiar faces have scattered or died, although I still catch KDKA on the car radio, deep in the night. The magic is gone, but I'll stick with it till it fades completely to hear again those little neighbouring town names: Belle Vernon, Castle Shannon, Blawnox, Sewickley – names that were ushering in life to me, holding promises of jobs and adventure. Those were all threshold names, places I couldn't have located on an Allegheny County map, but that nevertheless were part of my private empire, my homeland, the back of my hand, whose borders were marked by the snowy extremities of Wheeling, Altoona, Chambersburg and Cleveland.

Peter Humphries is about to leave this story, but not before he leaves his mark, freshly, on me again. His mother was divorced – *divorcée* was one of those words, probably the only one, that a 1952 Pittsburgh kid pronounced in a self-consciously French way, to imbue it with its full freight of accompanying *negligées* and *lingerie* and *brassières* and of other things that came off in the night and suggested a rich inner life – she had dates, and Peter often slept over with us on nights when she planned to stay away. Or didn't plan, but stayed away anyway. As a cocktail waitress, then hostess, she didn't come home till three or four in the morning anyway, then slept till noon.

He might have been the gateway to my adolescence, but as it turned out – that phrase again – he was merely the last of my childhood friends. In a life of sharp and inexplicable and unmendable breaks, I have a special feeling for these friends of a special time and place. They seem to me, all of them, including my parents, prisoners of peculiar moments, waving at me from ice floes as dark waters widen between us. I remember all of them sharply, for they never were given a chance to grow out and modify; they were forever the last way I saw them, just as Pittsburgh is, which is to say they are essences of themselves and of my own poor perception of them. Even so, they give a surer sense of my own continuity than anything I can conjure in myself.

Peter was predictably avid for sex. He was riveted on the female body, every part of it, in ways that only a deeply troubled boy can be: hating it, fearing it, desiring it. He found my ignorance of it and my indifference to learning about it from him something of an affront. It marked me as being just a kid, which I was.

Being with Peter, the only friend I had, was like standing at the tip of an enormous funnel; all the sexual knowledge available to pubescent, provincial Americans in 1952 was swirling past me, and not a precious drop was wasted, not with Peter and his mother nearby. I wasn't in their apartment that often – they had the cheaper, one-bedroom model – but every time I entered it I was struck by the fumes of something lurid. Peter's mother wasn't much older than thirty, her hair was black and ringleted, her body lean and firm, her habits and language loose and leering. She'd strung clotheslines across the living-room, and her entire stock of lingerie and negligees was usually on display. Her job demanded a lot of buttressing and tressing, as well as display and ornamentation. The apartment was always dark, always a den, in deference to her strange professional hours. I'd never seen so many bottles and lotions; things to drink, to spray, to paint, to rub in, to rub off; it shocked me, the absence of normal food, the exclusion of anything not related to her body, skin and hair. The sofa was draped in suggestive dresses still in dry-cleaner's plastic, and the kitchen had hosiery soaking in the sink and a slab of meat defrosting on the counter. Peter slept in the dining room, on a foldaway cot that he had to dispose of in a closet every morning. They had a large television set, a 'deal' she'd gotten from a motel close-out, but it didn't work.

What I responded to, of course, was the implicit savagery of that mother-son situation. She had nothing of the mother in her. She was a cruel woman who got by on lies about her youth, supported by candle-light and booze. A thirteen-year-old at home – who, as luck would have it, looked much older, with a jockey-like ropy body and tight, lined face of a child who wouldn't be growing much taller or broader – was the last thing in the world she would acknowledge as her own. They treated each other like husband and wife; he drank with her, gave her massages and sometimes crawled into bed with her.

There wasn't a time I visited when his mother was up and moving that I didn't leave that apartment without something shocking to me, some hunk of flesh observed or knowledge that would stimulate me like a laboratory rat in an uncontrolled experiment. She would excite a centre of consciousness, but leave me without completion or comprehension. A moment caught in the kitchen, with Mrs Humphries talking casually of 'ragging it' and needing some peace and quiet; of a man's voice muffled by the door to her bedroom shouting out, 'Hey, what the –?'

The most frightening moment didn't concern her at all. It was with Peter alone. 'Hey, want to see something? Look in here.' And before I could stop him, he was into his mother's clothes, underwear first, then the dresses and finally the make-up, all very professionally applied. We avoided each other for a few weeks after that. He'd let something drop.

My mother called her 'the slut'. Peter called her 'her' and 'she'. To have been the son of such a woman, to have absorbed the full blast without any shield (even grown men could take her only one night at a time) was a formula for disaster more potent than even my own. I envied him the nakedness of things in his life. His mother was to me, thanks to the luxury of deflection, like a pair of 3-D glasses on the world; things I couldn't have noticed in my mother or in my secretive parents stood in sharp relief thanks to her. And thanks to Peter, on those nights he'd shared my bed, I learned how women were built, what Kotexes were for, where 'it' went and how it got there. Thanks to Peter, I became a statistically normal American pre-teen, as judged by the Kinsey Foundation.

In most areas of development, I was keeping pace. Peter was the sexual guide, his mother the sexual quarry and my parents, the ultimately mysterious Reg and Hennie, were receding nicely from me as peers took over. A career based on my odd little passion for resolving distant images, for pulling in signals, was suggesting itself. It would be consistent with all this data to say that I grew up to become an astronomer, monitoring deep-dish radio telescope on a thin-aired mountaintop far from the murk of Pittsburgh. But even as children we are scouts; more daring and treacherous than the troops we lead, than the adults we become.

I have spoken of all the things I knew in 1952. What I didn't know was about to kill me. I died in 1952, not from my epilepsy or a fall from a sixth floor or an electric jolt or anything else from that world of Pittsburgh or Peter Humphries. These fragments stand out to me now, against a black background, and that seems to be the nature of childhood as it bleeds into adolescence: that we see faces without the lies and sympathies of self-protection, we can live events without antecedent or consequence. They appear tantalizingly sharp, but in a veil of snow and static: we can make them out, but then they fade and are no more.

My parents: Reg and Hennie Porter. My name is Philip. Phil Porter. Reg was working in a department store called Rosenbaum's in downtown Pittsburgh. It's been gone a quarter of a century now, so I'll not disguise any of these names. Names are treacherous anyway.

Reg was a good-looking man, about fifty, with dense white chest hair and forearms thick as Popeye's, hairy and with 'Amor Vincit' tatooed on one in a thin, unfurled banner under a starlet's face, neck and bare shoulders down to what promised to be indecent cleavage. He'd been married twice before, so far as I knew, and I'd found that out only when I overheard it. It didn't seem safe to ask if he had other children, though they'd hardly be kids. He might have married at twenty or less, so conceivably there were other Porters around, somewhere in New England, where he came from. He usually had the accent to prove it. But those kids could be thirty. My parents had been married eighteen years – I knew that from their number of anniversaries. I loved every aspect of that man.

If I could stop time, or stop narration, I would linger on the lean, graceful, grey-haired buxom figure of my mother (as she suddenly stands out to me) in the late summer of 1952. She was a woman softened by the grey in her hair, made younger by it (I don't remember her dark-haired, but I suspect she had looked almost masculine, the kind of young woman who must have a very handsome brother somewhere; a face that seems to find its resolution in the opposite sex). She hadn't married till thirty-two. Grey hair had finally focused her face, the way a beard might define an otherwise unspectacular set of features.

I've said enough. You will know already that the story is beginning to turn inside out. I had Oedipal longings – still do, doubtless, since I've never consciously considered them or worked them out – and my hours of staring into snowy screens, rejoicing with any faint signal, offers to me now a portrait of sublimation. There is sexual energy sparking over the gaps. And all my attempts at refining the images are doomed because the interference is built in: in my brain where blood vessels and nerve endings just don't quite reach, where some blunt or sharp object – in my case, a shard of bone – sliced through. And of the other connections to family and to place and even to language, I cannot speak at all. Those were things out on the street, outside of me entirely, about to knock on our door.

All right. People wonder what it's like to die, and since I've done it several hundred little-bad times and a few great convulsive big-bad times, and have died in other ways, too, I'll start small and build.

Dying is like this. You are twelve, coming back to the apartment after school. Picture it September, those scratchy days when the heat is up and school's not serious yet and the summer pursuits are still operative. I came home with a cherry sno-cone, about four o'clock. The front door was half open. Inside were half-packed boxes, all over the place, where selections of our things had been thrown in. My mother dashed from the kitchen to another opened box, a stack of china against her bosom, and eased them into the box and scrunched some pages of the *Post-Gazette* around them. She was a careful packer, and this was not careful packing. And because of my unexpected entrance, my shocked silence, her concentration, she did not see me. I caught her in expressions I'd never seen before; she was smaller, younger, sexier than she'd ever appeared before, all the more so for her obvious distress, or distraction, or anger – whatever indefinable thing it was. We'd moved many times before, and usually under bad conditions – to towns we didn't know and where we had no address. Those moves were chance things: pack up the car, flee a city and travel to a place where a job might be waiting. Then find an apartment after a few days in a squalid hotel, unpack, put the boy in school. We'd sometimes moved when rent was due; my father was so calm about it he could meet a landlord at the door, listen politely to his demand, reach in his pocket for the chequebook, saying all the time, 'Sure, sure', and then slap his forehead, 'God, forgot it!'

'That's okay, what about tomorrow?' the landlord would say.

'Right you are,' my father would say, 'first thing in the morning.' And two hours later we'd be at the outskirts of town, heading deeper into America.

My death was standing at the open door of my apartment, seeing my mother run from the kitchen clutching a stack of plates against her blouse and dropping them into a box, and thinking:

1. We're moving.
2. We're skipping.
3. Something terrible is happening.
4. Christ, my mother is a *sexy* woman.

a) On reflection, this last insight is tempered by the further insight that nearly any woman, when viewed unannounced, in the privacy of her living-room, is sexy. That is, the act of observing is sexy.

b) She legitimately was sexy. Her hair was up, but falling down, the grey and the black, and she was in slacks and one of my father's shirts, and she was looking good.

c) Sexiness, if I am now to lift it from any immediate context or application to any particular woman, is (for me) an appearance that borders on slovenliness. Sex will never embrace me in tennis shorts, in a bikini, or in any fetishistic combination of high heels and low neckline. Sex is the look that says, 'Help me out of these clothes', or shows that things she's wearing are a constriction, not an attraction.

On that late summer day in 1952, standing quietly and excitedly in the door of our apartment that was soon not to be our apartment, I had a seizure. When I woke up a few minutes later, my mother was holding the wooden spoon she used to keep me from biting my own tongue (what abuse that spoon had taken, over the years!). My mind was absolutely clean: I woke up remembering only that I knew something about my mother. And I knew something else: that this move was different from the others. In this one, the furniture was staying, but papers I'd never seen before were littering the floor. Papers in old leather folders with the crushed ribbons of official documents that had not been untied in a generation. When I could walk, she helped me back to the bedroom. She indicated that I should fall over my parents' double bed, but I ritually opened my own bedroom door.

Sitting on my bed was my father. I saw him in bright colour, the way only an epileptic can see the world, after an attack. I saw every pore, every hair, intensely sharp. I would not have recognized him on the street. He was crying, and it looked to me that he had been crying for hours and that he had nothing left to cry with. His shirt buttons were torn open, but his tie was still knotted, red silk over chest hair. His sleeves were rolled back, those massive arms lay helpless at his side and the cuff links were still stuck in the cuffs, and I worried that they'd fall out. My mother pushed me hard, out of my room and into theirs, and I was still groggy two hours later when she put two suitcases in my hands and told me to march quickly and quietly to the car, which was parked in the alley.

We headed north towards Buffalo and slipped through the middle of New York State all night long. He knew where he was going, though he didn't tell me. Around two o'clock in the morning he pulled into a large motel between Syracuse and Utica, waking me again, almost shaking me to make sure I was awake.

'Philip,' he said, all the time shaking me. 'Philip, until I tell you it's okay to talk, I don't want you to say a word. Not one word. Not even if someone talks to you, understand?'

'Even if things seem wrong,' my mother said. 'Even if you don't understand a thing.'

At three in the morning my father and I went prowling through the parking lot of that large motel while my mother slept in the car. I was scouting for a licence plate and a dollar bounty offered by my father. Finally I found one, on a black, pre-war Ford. My father stripped it of its plate – like Pennsylvania, they had only a rear plate – and put it on our car. Our plate was creased until it snapped, then buried. At five o'clock we were on the road again, over the Adirondacks, with my mother driving. They were talking now of 'the border', and the motels were flying two sets of flags, the American and a red British one, and ads were appearing for duty-free items. When the customs houses were in view, she pulled off to the side. My father took over. 'Tell him,' he told my mother and she turned around to face me.

'In a minute we'll be going to Canada. Canada is where your father and I come from.' She flashed some of those documents in front of me. 'We're going to Montreal. We have relatives in Montreal.'

I still had not spoken, could not speak.

'Our name will change when we go over the border. Forget all you ever knew about Porter. Our real name is Carry-A. Like this – see?' She showed me a plastic-coated green-framed card with an old picture of my father on it. I couldn't pronounce the name, but the letters bit into my brain. Réjean Carrier.

'What's my name?' I asked.

'I thought I told you to shut up,' said my father.

There were two cars in front of us. My father found a radio station playing strange music in a foreign language.

'You can be anything you want to be,' said my mother.

Grids and Doglegs

When I was sixteen I could spend whole evenings with a straight-edge, a pencil, and a few sheets of unlined construction paper, and with those tools I would lay out imaginary cities along twisting rivers or ragged coastlines. Centuries of expansion and division, terrors of fire and renewal, recorded in the primitive fiction of gaps and clusters, grids and doglegs. My cities were tangles; inevitably, like Pittsburgh. And as I built my cities, I'd keep the Pirates game on (in another notebook I kept running accounts of my team's declining fortunes – 'Well, Tony Bartirome, that knocks you down to .188' – the pre-game averages were never exact enough for me), and during the summers I excavated for the Department of Man, Carnegie Museum. Twice a week during the winter I visited the Casino Burlesque (this a winter pleasure, to counter the loss of baseball). I was a painter too, of sweeping subjects: my paleobotanical murals for the Devonian Fishes Hall are still a model for younger painter-excavators. (Are there others, still, like me, in Pittsburgh? This story is for them.) On Saturdays I lectured to the Junior Amateur Archaeologists and Anthropologists of Western Pennsylvania. I was a high school junior, my parents worked at their new store, and I was, obviously, mostly alone. In the afternoons, winter and summer, I picked up dirty clothes for my father's laundry.

I had – obviously, again – very few friends; there were not many boys like me. Fat, but without real bulk, arrogant but ridiculously shy. Certifiably brilliant but hopelessly unstudious, I felt unallied to even the conventionally bright honour-rollers in my suburban high school. Keith Godwin was my closest friend; I took three meals a week at his house, and usually slept over on Friday night.

Keith's father was a chemist with Alcoa; his mother a pillar of the local United Presbyterian Church, the Women's Club, and the University Women's chapter. The four children (all but Keith, the oldest), were models of charm, ambition and beauty. Keith was a moon-faced redhead with freckles and dimples – one would never suspect the depth of his cynicism – with just two real passions: the organ and competitive chess. I have seen him win five simultaneous blindfold games, ten-second moves – against tournament competition. We used to play at the dinner table without the board, calling out our moves while shovelling in the food. Years later, high-school atheism behind him, he enrolled in a Presbyterian seminary of Calvinist persuasions and is now a minister somewhere in California. He leads a number of extremist campaigns (crackpot drives, to be exact), against education, books, movies, minorities, pacifists – this, too, was a part of our rebellion, though I've turned the opposite way. But this isn't a story about Keith. He had a sister, Cyndy, one year younger.

She was tall, like her father, about five eight, an inch taller than I. Hers was the beauty of contrasts: fair skin, dark hair, grey eyes and the sharpness of features so common in girls who take after their fathers. Progressively I was to desire her as a sister, then wife and finally as lover; but by then, of course, it was too late. I took a fix on her, and she guided me through high school; no matter how far out I veered, the hope of eventually pleasing Cyndy drove me back.

In the summer of my junior year I put away the spade and my collection of pots and flints, and took up astronomy. There's a romance to astronomy, an almost courtly type of pain and fascination, felt by all who study it. The excitement: that like a character in the childhood comics, I could shrink myself and dismiss the petty frustrations of school, the indifference of Cyndy and my parents; that I could submit to points of light long burned-out and be rewarded with their cosmic tolerance of my obesity; that I could submit to the ridicule I suffered from the athletes in the lunch line, and to the Pirates' latest losing streak. I memorized all I could from the basic texts at Carnegie Library, and shifted my allegiance from Carnegie Museum to Buhl Planetarium. There was a workshop in the basement just getting going, started for teen-age telescope-builders, and I became a charter member.

Each week I ground out my lens; glass over glass through gritty water, one night a week for a least a year. Fine precise work, never my style, but I stuck with it while most of the charter enthusiasts fell away. The abrasive carborundum grew finer, month by month, from sand, to talc, to rouge – a single fleck of a coarser grade in those final months would have ploughed my mirror like a meteorite. Considering the winter nights on which I sacrificed movies and TV for that lens, the long streetcar rides, the aching arches, the insults from the German shop foreman, the meticulous scrubbing-down after each Wednesday session, the temptation to sneak upstairs for the 'Skyshow' with one of the chubby compliant girls – my alter egos – from the Jewish high school: *considering all that*, plus the all-important exclusiveness and recognition it granted, that superb instrument was a heavy investment to sell, finally, for a mere three hundred dollars. But I did, in the fine-polishing stage, because, I felt, I owed it to Cyndy. Three hundred dollars, for a new investment in myself.

Astronomy is the moral heavyweight of the physical sciences; it is a humiliating science, a destroyer of pride in human achievements, or shame in human failings. Compared to the vacant dimensions of space – of time, distance and temperature – what could be felt for Eisenhower's heart attack, Grecian urns, six million Jews, my waddle and shiny gabardines? My parents were nearing separation, their store beginning to falter – what could I care for their silence, their fights, the begging for bigger and bigger loans? The diameter of Antares, the Messier system, the swelling of space into uncreated nothingness – these things mattered because they were large, remote and perpetual. The Tammany Ring and follies of Hitler, Shakespeare and the Constitution were dust; the Andromeda galaxy was *worlds*. I took my meals out or with the Godwins, and I thought of these things as I struggled at chess with Keith and caught glimpses of Cyndy as she dried the dishes – if only I'd had dishes to dry!

The arrogance of astronomy, archaeology, chess, burlesque, baseball, science-fiction, everything I care for: humility and arrogance are often so close (the men I'm writing this for – who once painted murals and played in high school bands just to feel a part of something – they know); it's all the same feeling, isn't it? Nothing matters, except, perhaps, the proper irony. I had that irony once (I wish, in fact, I had it now), and it was something like this:

In the days of the fifties, each home room of each suburban high school started the day with a Bible reading and the pledge of allegiance to the flag. Thirty mumbling souls, one fervent old woman and me. It had taken me one night, five years earlier, to learn the Lord's Prayer backwards. I had looked up, as well, the Russian pledge and gotten it translated into English: this did for my daily morning ablutions. The lone difficulty had to do with Bible week, which descended without warning on a Monday morning with the demand that we, in turn, quote a snatch from the Bible. This is fine if your name is Zymurgy and you've had a chance to memorize everyone else's favourite, or the shortest verse. But I am a Dyer, and preceded often by Cohens and Bernsteins (more on that latter): Bible week often caught me unprepared. So it happened in the winter of my senior year that Marvin Bernstein was excused ('We won't ask Marvin, class, for he is of a different faith. Aren't you, Marvin?') And then a ruffian named Callahan rattled off a quick, 'For God so loved the world that he gave his only begotten Son ...' so fast that I couldn't catch it. A Sheila Cohen, whose white bra straps I'd stared at for one hour a day, five days a week, for three years – Sheila Cohen was excused. And Norman Dyer, I, stood. 'Remember, Norman,' said the teacher, 'I won't have the Lord's Prayer and the Twenty-second Psalm.' She didn't like Callahan's rendition either, and knew she'd get thirty more. From me she expected originality. I didn't disappoint.

'Om,' I said, and quickly sat. I'd learned it from the Vedanta, something an astronomer studies.

Her smile had frozen. It was her habit, after a recitation, to smile and nod and congratulate us with, 'Ah, yes, Revelations, a lovely choice, Nancy ...' But gathering her pluckiness she demanded, 'Just what is that supposed to mean, Norman?'

'Everything,' I said, with an astronomer's shrug. I was preparing a justification, something to do with more people in the world praying 'Om' than anything else, but I had never caused trouble before, and she decided to drop it. She called on my alphabetical shadow (a boy who'd stared for three years at my dandruff and flaring ears?), another Catholic, Dykes was his name, and Dykes this time, instead of following Callahan, twisted the knife a little deeper, and boomed out, 'Om ... amen!' Our teacher shut the Bible, caressed the marker, the white leather binding, and then read us a long passage having to do, as I recall, with nothing we had said.

That was the only victory of my high school years.

* * *

I imagined a hundred disasters a day that would wash Cyndy Godwin into my arms, grateful and bedraggled. Keith never suspected. My passion had a single outlet – the telephone. Alone in my parents' duplex, the television on, the Pirates game on, I would phone. No need to check the dial, the fingering was instinctive. Two rings at the Godwins'; if anyone but Cyndy answered, I'd hang up immediately. But with Cyndy I'd hold, through her perplexed 'Hellos?' till she queried, 'Susie, is that you?' 'Brenda?' 'Who is it, please?' and I would hold until her voice betrayed fear beyond the irritation. Oh, the pleasure of her slightly hysterical voice, 'Daddy, it's that *man* again,' and I would sniffle menacingly into the mouthpiece. Then I'd hang up and it was over; like a Pirates loss, nothing to do but wait for tomorrow. Cyndy would answer the phone perhaps twice a week. Added to the three meals a week I took with them, I convinced myself that five sightings or sounding a week would eventually cinch a marriage if I but waited for a sign she'd surely give me. She was of course dating a bright, good-looking boy a year ahead of me (already at Princeton), a conventional sort of doctor-to-be, active in Scouts, choir, sports and Junior Achievement, attending Princeton on the annual Kiwanis Fellowship. A very common type in our school and suburb, easily tolerated and easily dismissed. Clearly, a girl of Cyndy's sensitivity could not long endure his ministerial humour, his mere ignorance disguised as modesty. Everything about him – good looks, activities, athletics, piety, manners – spoke against him. In those years the only competition for Cyndy that I might have feared would have come from someone of my own circle. And that was impossible, for none of us had ever had a date.

And I knew her like a brother! Hours spent with her playing Scrabble, driving her to the doctor's for curious flaws I was never to learn about ... and, in the summers, accompanying the family to their cabin and at night hearing her breathing beyond a burlap wall ... Like a brother? Not even that, for as I write I remember Keith grabbing her on the stairs, slamming his open hands against her breasts, and Cyndy responding, while I ached to save her, 'Keith! What will Normie think?' And this went on for three years, from the first evening I ate with the Godwins when I was in tenth grade, till the spring semester of my senior year; Cyndy was a junior. There was no drama, no falling action, merely a sweet and painful stasis that I aggrandized with a dozen readings of

Cyrano de Bergerac, and a customizing of his soliloquies … 'This butt that follows me by half an hour … An ass, you say? Say rather a caboose, a dessert …' All of this was bound to end, only when I could break the balance.

We are back to the telescope, the three hundred well-earned dollars. Some kids I knew, Keith not included this time, took over the school printing press and ran off one thousand dramatic broadsheets, condemning a dozen teachers for incompetence and Lesbianism (a word that we knew meant more than 'an inhabitant of Lesbos,' the definition in our high-school dictionary). We were caught, we proudly confessed (astronomy again: I sent a copy to *Mad* magazine and they wrote back, *'Funny but don't get caught. You might end up working for a joint like this'*). The school wrote letters to every college that had so greedily accepted us a few weeks earlier, calling on them to retract their acceptance until we publicly apologized. Most of us did, for what good it did; I didn't – it made very little difference anyway, since my parents no longer could have afforded Yale. It would be Penn State in September.

I awoke one morning in April – a gorgeous morning – and decided to diet. A doctor in Squirrel Hill made his living prescribing amphetamines by the carload to suburban matrons. I lost thirty pounds in a month and a half, which dropped me into the ranks of the flabby underweights (funny, I'd always believed there was a *hard* me, under the fat, waiting to be sculpted out – there wasn't). And the pills (as a whole new generation is finding out) were marvellous: the uplift, the energy, the ideas they gave me! As though I'd been secretly rewired for a late but normal adolescence.

Tight new khakis and my first sweaters were now a part of the new-look Norman Dyer, which I capped one evening by calling the Arthur Murray Studios. I earned a free dance analysis by answering correctly a condescending question from their television quiz the night before. Then, with the three hundred dollars, I enrolled.

I went to three studio parties, each time with the enormous kid sister of my voluptuous instructress. That gigantic adolescent with a baby face couldn't dance a step (and had been brought along for me, I was certain), and her slimmed-down but still ample sister took on only her fellow teachers and some older, lonelier types, much to my relief. I wanted to dance, but not to be noticed. The poor big-little sister, whose name was Almajean, was dropping out of a mill-town high school in a year to become ... what? I can't guess, and she didn't know, even then. We drank a lot of punch, shuffled together when we had to, and I told her about delivering clothes, something she could respect me for, never admitting that my father owned the store.

But I knew what I had to do. For my friends there was a single event in our high school careers that *had*, above all, to be missed. We had avoided every athletic contest, every dance, pep rally, party – everything voluntary and everything mildly compulsory; we had our private insur- rections against the flag and God, but all that good work, all that consci- entious effort, would be wasted if we attended the flurry of dances in our last two weeks. The Senior Prom was no problem – I'd been barred because of the newspaper caper. But a week later came the Women's Club College Prom, for everyone going on to higher study (92 per cent always did). The pressure for a 100 per cent turnout was stifling. Even the teachers wore w c buttons so we wouldn't forget. Home room teachers managed to find out who was still uninvited (no one to give Sheila Cohen's bra a snap?). The College Prom combined the necessary exclusiveness and sophistication – smoking was permitted on the bal- cony – to have become the very essence of graduation night. And there was a special feature that we high schoolers had heard about ever since the eighth grade: the sifting of seniors into a few dozen booths, right on the dance floor, to meet local alums of their college-to-be, picking up a few fraternity bids, athletic money, while the band played a medley of privileged school songs. I recalled the pain I had felt a year before, as I watched Cyndy leave with her then-senior boyfriend, and I was still there, playing chess, when they returned around 2 A.M. for punch.

It took three weeks of aborted phone calls before I asked Cyndy to the College Prom. She of course accepted. Her steady boyfriend was already at Princeton and ineligible. According to Keith, he'd left instruc- tions: nothing serious. What did *he* know of seriousness, I thought, making my move. I bought a dinner jacket, dancing shoes, shirt, links, studs, cummerbund; and I got ten dollars' spending money from my astonished father. I was seventeen, and this was my first date.

Cyndy was a beautiful *woman* that night; it was the first time I'd seen her consciously glamorous. The year before she'd been a girl, well turned-out, but a trifle thin and shaky. But not tonight! Despite the glistening car and my flashy clothes, my new near-mesomorphy, I felt like a worm as I slipped the white orchid corsage around her wrist. (I could have had a bosom corsage; when the florist suggested it, I nearly ran from the shop. What if I jabbed her, right *there*?) And I could have cried at the trouble she'd gone to, for *me:* her hair was up, she wore glittering earrings and a pale sophisticated lipstick that made her lips look chapped. And, mercifully, flat heels. The Godwin family turned out for our departure, so happy that I had asked her, so respectful of my sudden self-assurance. Her father told me to stay out as long as we wished. Keith and the rest of my friends were supposedly at the movies, but had long been planning, I knew, for the milkman's matinee at the Casino Burlesque. I appreciated not having to face him – wondering, in fact, how I ever would again. My best-kept secret was out (oh, the ways they have of getting us kinky people straightened out!); but she was mine tonight, the purest, most beautiful, the *kindest* girl I'd ever met. And for the first time, for the briefest instant, I connected her to those familiar bodies of the strippers I knew so well, and suddenly I felt that I knew what this dating business was all about and why it excited everyone so. I understood how thrilling it must be actually to touch, and kiss, and look at naked, a beautiful woman whom you loved, and who might touch you back.

The ballroom of the Women's Club was fussily decorated; dozens of volunteers had worked all week. Clusters of spotlights strained through the sagging roof of crepe (the lights blue-filtered, something like the Casino), and the couples in formal gowns and dinner jackets seemed suddenly worthy of college and the professional lives they were destined to enter. A few people stared at Cyndy and smirked at me, and I began to feel a commingling of pride and shame, mostly the latter.

We danced a little – rumbas were my best – but mainly talked, drinking punch and nibbling the rich sugar cookies that her mother, among so many others, had helped to bake. We talked soberly, of my enforced retreat from the Ivy League (not even the car stealers and petty criminals on the fringe of our suburban society had been treated as harshly as I), of Keith's preparation for Princeton. Her grey eyes never left me. I talked of other friends, two who were leaving for a summer in Paris, to polish their French before entering Yale. Cyndy listened to it all, with her cool hand on my wrist. 'How I wish Keith had taken someone tonight!' she exclaimed.

Then at last came the finale of the dance: everyone to the centre of the floor, everyone once by the reviewing stand, while the orchestra struck up a medley of collegiate tunes. 'Hail to Pitt!' cried the president of the Women's Club, and Pitt's incoming freshmen, after whirling past the bandstand, stopped at an adjoining booth, signed a book and collected their name tags. The rousing music blared on, the fight songs of Yale and Harvard, Duquesne and Carnegie Tech, Penn State, Wash and Jeff, Denison and Wesleyan ...

'Come on, Normie, we can go outside,' she suggested. We had just passed under the reviewing stand, where the three judges were standing impassively. Something about the King and Queen; nothing I'd been let in on. The dance floor was thinning as the booths filled. I broke the dance-stride and began walking her out, only to be reminded by the w c president, straining above 'Going Back to Old Nassau', to keep on danc-ing, please. The panel of judges – two teachers selected by the students, and Mr Hartman, husband of the club's president – were already on the dance floor, smiling at the couples and poking their heads into the clogged booths. Cyndy and I were approaching the doors, near the bruisers in my Penn State booth. One of the algebra teachers was racing toward us, a wide grin on his florid face, and Cyndy gave my hand a tug. 'Normie,' she whispered, 'I think something wonderful is about to hap-pen.'

The teacher was with us, a man much shorter than Cyndy, who panted, 'Congratulations! You're my choice.' He held a wreath of roses above her head, and she lowered her head to receive it. 'Ah – what is your name?'

'Cyndy Godwin,' she said. 'Mr Esposito.'

'Keith Godwin's sister?'

'Yes.'

'And how are you, Norman – or should I ask?' Mr Wheeler, my his-tory teacher, shouldered his way over to us; he held out a bouquet of yellow mums. 'Two out of three,' he grinned, 'that should just about do it.'

'Do what?' I asked. I wanted to run, but felt too sick. Cyndy squeezed my cold hand; the orchid nuzzled me like a healthy dog. My knees were numb, face burning.

'Cinch it,' said Wheeler. 'King Dyer.'

'If Hartman comes up with someone else, then there'll be a vote,' Esposito explained. 'If he hasn't been bribed, then he'll choose this girl too and that'll be it.'

I have never prayed harder. Wheeler led us around the main dance floor, by the rows of chairs that were now empty. The musicians suspended the Cornell evening hymn to enable the wc president to announce dramatically, in her most practised voice, 'The Queen approaches.'

There was light applause from the far end of the floor. Couples strained from the college booths as we passed, and I could hear the undertone, '… he's a brain in my biology class, Norman something-or-other, but I don't know her …' I don't *have* to be here, I reminded myself. No one made me bring her. I could have asked one of the girls from the Planetarium who respected me for my wit and memory alone – or I could be home like any other self-respecting intellectual, in a cold sweat over *I Led Three Lives*. The Pirates were playing a twi-nighter and I could have been out there at Forbes Field in my favourite right-field upperdeck, where I'm an expert … why didn't I ask her out to a baseball game? Or I could have been where I truly belonged, with my friends down at the Casino Burlesque....

'You'll lead the next dance, of course,' Wheeler whispered. Cyndy was ahead of us, with Esposito.

'Couldn't someone else?' I said. 'Maybe you – why not you?' Then I said with sudden inspiration, 'She's not a senior. I don't think she's eligible, do you?'

'Don't worry, don't worry, Norman.' I had been one of his favourite pupils. 'Her class hasn't a thing to do with it, just her looks. And Norman' – he smiled confidentially – 'she's an extraordinarily beautiful girl.'

'Yeah,' I agreed, had to. I drifted to the stairs by the bandstand. 'I'm going to check anyway,' I said. I ran to Mrs Hartman herself. 'Juniors aren't eligible to be Queen, are they? I mean, she'll get her own chance next year when she's going to college, right?'

Her smile melted as she finally looked at me; she had been staring into the lights, planning her speech. 'Is her escort a senior?'

'Yes,' I admitted, 'but *he* wasn't chosen. Anyway, he's one of those guys who were kept from the Prom. By rights I don't think he should even be here.'

'I don't think this has ever come up before.' She squinted into the footlights, a well-preserved woman showing strain. 'I presume you're a class officer.'

'No, I'm her escort.'

'Her *escort*? I'm afraid I don't understand. Do I know the girl?'

'Cyndy Godwin?'

'You don't mean Betsy Godwin's girl? Surely I'm not to take the prize away from that lovely girl, just because – well, just because *why* for heaven's sake?'

The bandleader leaned over and asked if he should start the 'Miss America' theme. Mrs Hartman fluttered her hand. And then from the other side of the stand, the third judge, Mr Hartman, hissed to his wife. 'Here she is,' he beamed.

'Oh, dear me,' began Mrs. Hartman.

'A vote?' I suggested. 'It has to be democratic.'

The second choice, a peppy redhead named Paula, innocently followed Mr Hartman up the stairs and was already smiling like a winner. She was a popular senior, co-vice-president of nearly everything. Oh, poise! Glorious confidence! Already the front rows were applauding the apparent Queen, though she had only Mr Hartman's slender cluster of roses to certify her. Now the band started up, the applause grew heavy, and a few enthusiasts even whistled. Her escort, a union leader's son, took his place behind her, and I cheerfully backed off the bandstand, joining Cyndy and the teachers at the foot of the steps. Cyndy had returned her flowers, and Mr Wheeler was standing dejectedly behind her, holding the bouquet. The wreath dangled from his wrist.

'I feel like a damn fool,' he said.

'That was very sweet of you, Normie,' Cyndy said, and kissed me hard on the cheek.

'I just can't get over it,' Wheeler went on. 'If anyone here deserves that damn thing, it's you. At least take the flowers.'

I took them for her. 'Would you like to go?' I asked. She took my arm and we walked out. I left the flowers on an empty chair.

I felt more at ease as we left the school and headed across the street to the car. It was a cool night, and Cyndy was warm at my side, holding my arm tightly. 'Let's have something to eat,' I suggested, having practised the line a hundred times, though it still sounded badly acted. I had planned the dinner as well; *filet mignon* on toast at a classy restaurant out on the highway. I hadn't planned it for quite so early in the night, but even so, I was confident. A girl like Cyndy ate out perhaps once or twice a year, and had probably never ordered *filet*. I was more at home in a fancy restaurant than at a family table.

'I think I'd like that,' she said.

'What happened in there was silly – just try to forget all about it,' I said. 'It's some crazy rule or something.'

We walked up a side street, past a dozen cars strewn with crepe.

'It's not winning so much,' she said. 'It's just an embarrassing thing walking up there like that and then being left holding the flowers.'

'There's always next year.'

'Oh, I won't get it again. There are lots of prettier girls than me in my class.'

An opening, I thought. So easy to tell her that she was a queen, deservedly, any place. But I couldn't even slip my arm around her waist, or take her hand that rested on my sleeve.

'Well, I think you're really pretty.' And I winced.

'Thank you, Norman.'

'Prettier than anyone I've ever –'

'I understand,' she said. Then she took my hand and pointed it above the streetlights. 'I'll bet you know all those stars, don't you, Normie?'

'Sure.'

'You and Keith – you're going to be really something someday.'

We came to the car; I opened Cyndy's door and she got in. 'Normie?' she said, as she smoothed her skirt before I closed the door, 'could we hurry? I've got to use the bathroom.'

I held the door open a second. *How dare she,* I thought, that's not what she's supposed to say. This is a date; you're a queen, my own queen. I looked at the sidewalk, a few feet ahead of us, then said suddenly, bitterly, 'There's a hydrant up there. Why don't you use it?'

I slapped the headlights as I walked to my side, hoping they would shatter and I could bleed to death.

'That wasn't a very nice thing to say, Norman,' she said as I sat down.

'I know.'

'A girl who didn't know you better might have gotten offended.'

I drove carefully, afraid now on this night of calamity that I might be especially accident-prone. It was all too clear now, why she had gone with me. Lord, protect me from a too-easy forgiveness. In the restaurant parking lot, I told her how sorry I was for everything, without specifying how broad an everything I was sorry for.

'You were a perfect date,' she said. 'Come on, let's forget about everything, ok?'

Once inside, she went immediately to the powder room. The hostess, who knew me, guided me to a table at the far end of the main dining room. She would bring Cyndy to me. My dinner jacket attracted some attention; people were already turning to look for my date. I sat down; water was poured for two, a salad bowl appeared. When no one was looking, I pounded the table. *Years of this,* I thought: slapping head-lights, kicking tables, wanting to scream a memory out of existence, wanting to shrink back into the stars, the quarries, the right-field stands – things that could no longer contain me. A smiling older man from the table across the aisle snapped his fingers and pointed to his cheek, then to mine, and winked. 'Lipstick!' he finally whispered, no longer smiling. I had begun to wet the napkin when I saw Cyndy and the hostess approaching – and the excitement that followed in Cyndy's wake. I stood to meet her. She was the Queen, freshly beautiful, and as I walked to her she took a hanky from her purse and pressed it to her lips. Then in front of everyone, she touched the moistened hanky to my cheek, and we turned to take our places.

The Seizure

We are talking of southern Ohio, southwestern Pennsylvania, that segregated blade of West Virginia that inserts itself between the East and the Middle West. Where are we? North? East? Midwest? You cannot say. What exactly are these people? A college boy on Christmas holidays, working reluctantly at his father's store; a giant black man in a green uniform, standing over his boss, hammer in hand, a look so hurt and menacing on his face that – let us say – a state trooper suddenly bursting into the store would fire first and be pardoned later; the boss, a tight little man, bald, moustached, robust in the hairy way of the short and bald. (You've seen him a thousand times in clothing stores, used-car lots, hotels. Cigars, rings on pinky, gold watch band gleaming on a hairy wrists.) The name is Malick. There are Mullicks in India, Maliks in Russia and the Middle East, Meliks in Egypt, Mallochs in Scotland, Malicks universally in the garment trade. Even the boss traces nothing back further than two generations. His faith was inherited: the shortest, darkest Presbyterian in the town of his birth. Uncles of his in larger cities had kept a complicated faith, with demanding rituals and obscure saints.

They are stringing a wire, the giant driver and the short, sweating businessman.

Upstairs, a woman in high heels greets a customer.

Offstage, alone in a suburban home back in the hills, Margaret Malick – Justin's mother, the boss's wife – breaks eggs for an omelet. She worries about a phone call, whether to uncradle the receiver now, or to answer it when it rings.

Expected any time now, from the library, Justin. Called Judd, a name he has hated since its first corruption into Jug and its later similarity to the Jeds, Jebs and Jeps in the hills around him. Mornings in the library thirty miles away, afternoons in the store helping out. He lives for the school year to end, when he will decamp to France for his junior year. Justin Malick, six feet two and consumptively thin, with the olive complexion of his father and his mother's massive bones, will make a perfect Parisian Arab. He can see his name tacked up on a splintered door: *Justin Maliq*. He can picture himself in a left bank café reading, nervously puffing a rancid Gauloise. There is a *tabac* in Wheeling, thirty miles west, that sells Gauloises, Gitanes and Celtiques. He's added a new word from this morning's reading: *fricoteur,* a procurer of illicit delectables. In Wheeling, a *Gitane* pimp. Near-compensation for the unpleasant duties at hand.

The mind of Delman, who holds the hammer over the boss's head, who drives the truck and delivers the goods, is vastly more complex than Junior's, or the boss's. To the son, it seems merely a dark humid cellar; littered, earthen, sealed upon itself; slow, fat flies buzzing incessantly against the screens. There is a dripping from somewhere.

Once, when he was just a kid, Delman saw a bunch of pictures in *Life* of what the Japanese did, first thing after entering a Chinese village. Got the mayor and all the local bosses, all the big-shot landowners and all the men between ten and fifty and a few girls to spice it up, and put them in a building and set it on fire. Soldiers sat around with machine guns covering the exits. Mowed them down as they came pouring out, shirts on fire, hands up. *Ooo-eee,* some fucking Bar-B-Q. *Banzai!* Few years later *Life* got the shots of Mao hitting Shanghai, and then it was the big-shot landlords all over again, down on their knees with their wives and kids, hands tied to paddles behind. All of the kids with their hands tied, bending over. One second there's a kid with his hair a little sticking up the way Chinese hair is always sticking up, in a clean white shirt he probably took out of the drawer that morning not ever knowing it would be his last one, and his feet in good sandals and his mouth open to say something to his father who's kneeling at the next paddle (saying *what,* he'd wondered as a young man: 'Daddy, is it going to hurt?' 'Daddy, tell them to stop it ...' 'Daddy, are they really going to shoo –') and a second later his brains are coming out of his mouth and his hair is plastered on his father's shirt. First time he saw it, he got a headache. But he never forgot.

'Just loop it over the doorframe, Delman,' says the boss. At six six, Delman's got about a foot on the boss. 'I'm sure as hell grateful she thought of this,' Malick says. 'Some kind of time-saver, huh? All those trips you used to have to make up from the warehouse – think of the time you'll save! She figured two hours a week – *easy* two hours a week. And think of all the work you'll get done without us bothering you till we call.'

Ooo-eee, just think.

'Hey – guess what it cost, the whole rig. Take a guess.'

'I'm sure I'd be wrong.'

'Go on, try.'

'Oh, I'm sure I'd guess way too high.'

'Nail it in up there, Delman. God, you're some kind of giant, aren't you? What d'ya go – six four? Six five? You should've played basketball, Delman, they're always looking for guys like you. Now come on, take a guess.'

I played, I played. All-state twenty-five years ago, driving a truck all over those Jap-held islands a year later. Been driving ever since. 'You want a guess, Mr Malick? o K. Here's a guess. I'd say shopping smartly you can pick up a two-way intercom and about half a mile of cable for five ninety-five.' And you could see the boss wilting a little, as if you'd dropped the hammer accidentally on his head.

'Dammit, Delman, you're not stupid. Use your head and guess again.'

'*Ten* dollars?' Eyes wide.

'For your information, you're holding the latest intercom on the market. German-made, from Office Outfitters. Finest on the market. Twenty-nine bucks complete. Can't beat that. Now what I want to know is how come we didn't think of it before, huh?'

'Well, I don't remember being asked, Mr Malick –'

'*We* – how come Mrs Malick, how come she never thought of it, since she's suddenly so concerned about the store?'

'Mrs Malick always walked down and got me herself.'

'That's just like her. Walk down and leave the floor empty for ten minutes. That's what I call smart. How come it takes Mrs Simmons one week on the job to tell me we need an intercom? I swear to God that woman takes more interest in this store than anyone we've ever had.' The boss looks up lovingly at the sound of heels tapping their way back to the office. The squeal of casters as she settles again into his office chair. Delman keeps on nailing, the boss keeps on praising. Upstairs, Mrs Simmons is placing a call. 'She's smart, Delman. God, it frightens me how smart she is. Learned the whole routine, *everything,* perfect in a week. In a week! You know I've had experienced furniture men come to me and ask me where I found her. "Don't let that one get away, Jerry" – that's what they say. And she's got energy. Sells like three experienced men.'

'She's got that good experience all right.' And Delman remembers where they found her – in an ad: 'WANTED: AGGRESSIVE SALESWOMAN FOR THRIVING SUBURBAN FIRM.' When Mrs Simmons said 'firm' you could feel her squeezing it; you could feel it break in her hand.

Mrs Simmons: you've seen her too. Behind cosmetic counters in overcooled Florida drugstores. Receptionist in a cocktail lounge. She is sitting in the office, dialling Margaret Malick. Her voice is honeyed; hair, eyelids, lips and nails all frosted. Figure, at forty-odd, stunning. A few wrinkles under the chin, around the mouth. One can imagine her, under the make-up, a girl of twenty from the hills around here, gawky. Uncertain. Accented. Tough and bony. One, two, three husbands later she owns a home, a bank account, a brutal confidence. The last husband has made her a widow; the first a mother; the second polished the diamond he'd taken away, only to lose her to an older, richer and stuffier man.

A voice, weak and tentative: 'Hello?'

'Hello, Margaret. How *are* you, dear?'

'I've asked you never to call. I've warned you. I'll tell Jerry.'

'But *that's* why I'm calling, Margaret. If you have a message for Jerry, why don't you just give it to me? Now, the reason I'm calling is so you won't be worrying about tonight, all right? Jerry will be taking me out to dinner after we close, and I just don't see *how* we can be free before midnight, all right? And I'd be positively *frantic* if the roads get all icy and I had to send him home all by himself.'

'Please –'

'I mean, I absolutely couldn't forgive myself if I was to blame for anything happening to my boss, right?'

'Stop – all I want is for you to stop. Please. Stop.'

'Well, Mrs Malick, if *that's* the way you feel about a friendly little phone call, then I can certainly understand all the things Jerry tells me about you. I didn't *want* to believe them, but –'

She waits two minutes, then dials again.

Mrs Simmons was out to lunch when Judd arrived from the library. The intercom had been installed. Delman and his father were in the office going over a file. 'You're late,' his father said. 'The deputy's already here.'

There had been a cop car in the parking lot; something suspicious about its studious plain-blackness had made him look a second time. The driver, in khaki, had been on the two-way radio. Then another patrol car – this one decked out in white doors, township crest, and revolving light – had pulled into the parking lot, and the two cars had rubbed against each other as the deputies talked. Like copulating worms, he'd thought at the time, each pointed in the opposite direction.

'o k, if we're ready now. You remember Szafransky?'

'She the lady with the tattoo?' Delman asked.

'What tattoo? He bought a ninety-six-inch sofa, a bedroom suite, lamps, rugs and three tables. Hutch, sideboard, six chairs.'

'On her elbow. Ooo-eee, a little blue star right smack on her elbow.'

'Well, we're repossessing on sheriff's orders and he's sent a deputy to go out with you. I want you to take out every stick of furniture on that order, got it? And make sure you get the louse's signature when you leave.'

'Right. Get the deputy's signature.'

'Cut it out. You may think it's funny, and *him*, he's probably laughing to himself seeing his old man losing money, but I've got four thousand dollars tied up in that son of a bitch. Cheating a man who gives you credit – that's the lowest thing in the book. A rotter, that's all. By God, I'd rather be selling to niggers than bohunks like him. No offence, Delman. Prison's too good, too good. I want you in and out of there as quick as possible and if he tries anything, let the deputy handle it. Deputy's costing me fifty bucks an hour.'

'What do you mean – *if he tries anything?*' asked Judd.

'I mean exactly what I said. If you touch anything but the furniture, it's assault. If they touch you, it's interference. I don't want either one of you saying a word to those people, got it?'

'Gotcha.'

'I know *you* won't. It's the boy I'm worried about. He's good at some things, but it would be like sending his mother in there and trying to come out with anything. Just try to get it into your head that this is business and those people got charity from me and they abused it and try not

69

to be like some kind of goddamn social worker when you deal with bohunks, o k? And if the merchandise is damaged, I want you to write out a description on the spot and the deputy will sign it. He's got the forms.'

The deputy tailgated in the unmarked car. Delman thought of other men he'd sat with in the cabs of delivery trucks: white and black, college boys, drunks, racists, ex-cons, weaklings, queers. Relatives, scabs, junkies. All the faces and all the names he'd had to learn, all the home towns, all their bitches with the world. All the waste. But no matter what else, they all looked right for the job. They dressed right. They sat right in the cab. They looked capable and barely strong enough. If they talked, it was about the right things for delivering furniture. But Junior sat hunched against the door with both legs up on the seat between them. Reading a French book and cutting the pages. Delman had warned him when they left: look, this ain't no T-Bird with kiddie-locks, sit straight! Truck doors can give way, especially when your old man buys them third-hand and they're already dented. All I need is losing Junior out the door when I'm driving.

'So, how're they treating you up there?'

'They leave me alone. After your freshman year you can do pretty much whatever you like.'

They turned off the state highway, onto a county road that dipped towards a creek and bridge. If you go one way, curling up along the ridges and back down a valley or two, you come to some expensive homes, the boss's among them. But if you stick with the county road down along the 'run', you come to a string of dead-end villages clinging to a railroad spur that used to carry coal. The road is snowbanked and cindered, barely covering the abandoned cars. The high ridge beyond the creek is white and studded with black trees. Good hunting, once. The road narrows to a one-lane bridge, then leads in front of a cluster of shanties at the other end. The water is black, with snow-topped rocks in the middle. A couple of old women in babushkas slog along the broken sidewalk. There is a discount gas station marked with a rusted, hand-painted billboard, 'GAS 26.9', next to a food store that looks closed.

'God, this is foreign,' said Judd. 'It's like a painting, you know?'

In front of the store stood a state historical marker, but Delman didn't slow down.

'What's the marker for?'

Delman knew it well but said only, 'You don't like to lose a single edifying experience, do you?' Then he laughed, 'Ooo-eee, as we knee-grows say, you're somethin' else, Junior. Somethin' else.' It marked the deepest northern penetration of Confederate troops, where a raiding party and some local copperheads linked up in 1862 for their own special reasons and raided this hole of a then-black hamlet called Enoch. They burned it down because by 1862 it was 100 per cent black and free although just a handful had their legal papers. After gutting the town they took some people back over the river into Virginia and Kentucky, while the local citizens contented themselves with rape and murder and scattering the rest of the blacks into the hills. Those were Delman's people, hill-niggers that roamed free, shooting coons and squirrels until basketball and the war intervened. By then the Polacks had come and taken over whatever was left. And with the Polacks the whole thing hadn't changed in forty years. Of course the historical marker didn't say a thing about blacks and Polacks. It read: 'FIRST ENGAGEMENT WITH CONFEDERATE FORCES ON UNION SOIL, Burning of Enoch, 1862.'

The Szafransky house was partly up the ridge and connected to the creek road by a driveway lined with painted rocks and red reflectors. It was too soupy for the truck, so Delman parked a little off the road, making sure to block the drive. They waited in the cab for the deputy to come around. He was a small sallow man with a high husky voice that sounded Deep South. Half the voices in this region are Southern. He squinted; his uniform was soiled.

'This it? Up that drive?'

'That's where I brung it last spring. They could have moved since, but that's the place.'

'Well, the residence appears occupied,' said the deputy. 'Smoke in the chimney. Let's get it over with.'

'We'll just wait here for the all-clear, seeing's how you got the badge.'

The deputy squinted, cocked his head. 'No, sir, you get on down and come up there with me. This here's your mess, not mine. I'll be right behind if there's any ruckus. And don't think you can start giving me orders, neither.'

In front of the cottage stood a rusty mailbox with 'szafransky' painted in lower case. Delman snickered and pointed it out. 'Reckon they been reading their e e cummings?' he asked, then turned his head quickly as though he hadn't said a thing. *Oh, yes, there is some shit I will not eat, and that was the truest poem anyone had ever written.* Junior was walking with one eye on the house, slightly behind him, because this was mountaineer country where everyone hunted and every so often, especially near Christmas, a man would shoot his family and then a couple of neighbours and barricade himself inside to shoot it out with the state patrol. But they reached the door without a movement from inside.

Judd looked around the yard and kept away from the screen door. Delman rattled it. The summer porch was crammed with wooden tables, smashed cane chairs, and crushed toys under a dusting of snow. There was a main door beyond, but the screen door was latched.

'Deputy, open up!' the little man shouted, but his voice didn't carry. He kicked the screen door hard against the frame.

Pump a few rounds into the kitchen, thought Delman.

A child lifted the curtain on the inner door. Then a tall, wide-shouldered man with a run-over blond crewcut, dressed in overalls and a red flannel shirt, opened the door. He smelled of unbrushed teeth. He said nothing, but his eyes settled on Judd.

'Well, I done my piece,' said the deputy. 'Get it over with if you're going to do it.'

Judd's voice came out clear. 'We're from Malick's. The deputy has the papers for picking up the furniture.'

'What kind of papers gives you the right to come barging in my house and taking off my furniture in Christmas week?'

Meubles gagés: French kept occurring to him at the oddest times. He couldn't think of it in English. It was a good Célinesque word, something he'd been reading that morning. 'We're seizing the furniture against your unpaid account. You were sent a notice.'

Szafransky was joined by his wife. She had a mannish face, but a narrow body, and she linked one arm with her husband's, keeping the other on her hip. The effect was insolent and almost exciting. She looked suspicious and submissive, like a captured woman in occupied territory.

'Let's see them papers you got,' said Szafransky, walking over the broken toys to the screen door. His hands, Judd noticed, were red and scaly, the stubby fingers stretching the skin like boiled Polish sausages. He made a show of studying the papers, then said, 'Reckon it's legal.'

Inside, Judd smelled cabbage and watched the kids scatter. The ceilings were low; only the deputy fitted in. They were like a giant tribe in undersized quarters; everyone stooped, and Judd wanted to shield his head from something falling. Two boys and two girls pointed at Delman behind his back.

'Son of a bitch didn't leave us no time to pay up,' Szafransky told the deputy. 'Been out of work four month.' The place was steaming hot, the children coughed as they whispered, and piles of toys, dishes, papers, and clothes littered the space between the television and the miniature chairs.

Quelle porcherie!

'Son of a bitch sends me a Merry Christmas card saying he's taking us to court, and me with four kids. Where'm I getting a fancy lawyer can standt up to Mr J. Fucking Malick? Trusts me for a couple thousand dollar then he takes it back 'cause I miss five hundred. Make sense to you?'

'I don't make the rules,' said the deputy.

I do, thought Judd. *God help me.*

The dining-room table, the chairs and a hutch were already beyond repair. Delman was writing it down. Mrs Szafransky slowly cleared the table of milk cartons, cereal bowls, paste, and colouring books. Globs of glue had blistered off the finish; the milk rings were plastic-hard. The chairs had nail gouges from the children's run-over shoes, and the fancy knobs and railings of the colonial hutch had broken off. Delman stacked the three side chairs and took them to the truck.

'Well, I reckon a cup of coffee won't hurt nobody,' said Mrs Szafransky to the deputy. 'I know you ain't a part of this.'

'Don't put yourself out none.'

In a minute she brought a kettle of boiling water and a green glass mug with a spoonful of instant coffee in the bottom. The kettle and cup went directly on the table. 'Reckon no need to put a place mat down is there?' she said and left a generous ring of boiling water around the cup.

'You?'

'No, thank you.'

'Better watch who you're talking to,' said the deputy. He smiled over the lip of the cup. 'That's there fine young man you're talking to is none other than the boss's son. That right there is Mister Malick Junior.'

'Funny,' she said, 'I kinda had the other one figgered for the boss's son.'

The deputy, blinking and smiling, took a long loud suck on his coffee, making it sound as thick as soup. Delman came back from the truck.

'Got in much hunting yet?' Szafransky asked the deputy. 'Got me a nine-point buck back in the freezer.'

'Just some squirrel is all.'

'Looks like good coon shootin' round here,' said Szafransky.

'Ain't never seen a bigger one,' said the deputy.

'Just tip that hutch over,' said Delman to Judd. 'I can get the rest of it on my back.'

'Well trained, too,' said Szafransky.

'That's a plenty good helper you brung along, mister,' said the deputy. Then he added to Szafransky, 'Didn't you hear what I told your missus? That-there is Mister Malick Junior.'

Szafransky squinted, then asked, 'Reckon he'd come back later without his nigger?'

'Don't hardly think so.'

'Sort of a queer-lookin' little cocksucker, ain't he?' he asked his wife.

'You leaving these people a pot to piss in, boy?' asked the deputy.

'You have the list.'

'Seems like damn near everything to me.'

'Look – me and the wife can use some fresh air after cocksuck and the nigger been here. Gotta buy us a Christmas tree and some furniture down to the shopping centre. Just close up the house when you're done.' Szafransky passed close to Judd, who wanted to run. He pinched Judd's chin in his red sausage fingers. Judd trembled. Szafransky cleared his throat. 'Naw – not this time. You ain't even worth spittin' on, you know?' His wife got her coat and scarf. 'You kids be good and don't touch the stove, hear? We'll be back direct.' They walked down the driveway, past the furniture truck and the deputy's car. Judd heard laughter.

Judd began stripping the bed. Parts of the sheets stuck to the mattress, then ripped away. The odours made him dizzy, the heat and closeness, the essence of the Szafransky life. If all this afternoon's business had a meaning, it lay somehow in these sheets. But what it was, exactly, he didn't know. The deputy, smirking, stood beside him. He's here to protect them, Judd thought.

'The bed goes too, huh?' he asked. 'Kid's beds too? I seen you watching the lady – wouldn't you just like to settle out of court, huh? Wouldn't you and the nigger like to knock off a piece of that, huh?'

Judd folded the sheets, so cold and damp, and dropped them with the pillows on the floor. 'Maybe if I pulled a gun on Szafransky, so's you and the nigger could have a go at her, nice and safe and legal, huh?' There were spots on the mattress so dark that they looked like grease puddles. The buttons had all been sprung and the welt was pulling loose. The *use* it must have had!

'But then I guess it don't bother you none, does it, taking their bed right out from under them. I mean look at the mattress – it ain't worth a nickel now 'cept maybe for charging admission. What about it, boy – a nickel a sniff for all your friends? Whang off on it for a dollar?'

Delman came back and started knocking the bedframe down. He and the deputy exchanged man-of-the-world, interracial smiles at the state of the mattress. *Me too,* Judd wanted to shout, *don't you think I know? Don't you think I can imagine them at night, the two of them in the middle, on the sides, sitting, rocking, pumping, bucking…*

'You was giving her the eye too – I seen that,' the deputy said as Delman carried the frames past him.

'Can't control myself with them tattooed women,' he laughed back. 'You catch that little blue star just above her elbow? Ooo-eee!'

Judd and Delman picked up the box spring and carried it out. Stuck to its underside were pairs of undershorts and dozens of clumps of pink tissue paper. Judd started to pry them off with his pen, but Delman stopped him. 'Your daddy said he wanted everything, and by God I'm going to give it to him.'

Each time they carried out a new article, Judd prepared himself for something violent. A rifle shot from the garage, Szafransky lunging with a butcher knife. Delman didn't seem at all concerned and he should know. Would Delman have fought, or even killed, under these same conditions? He wondered. What if some whites came to take his Italian Provincial bedroom suite? Or would Delman have repossessed from Negroes? Would Negroes have let him? And why such sudden acquiescence from a man like Szafransky? When can you predict? When can you take furniture from an unemployed hunter and walk out unharmed, and when is some sleepy gentle schoolteacher going to blow your head off? There was something so vulnerable in the testimony of Kleenex parachutes, that he wanted to return the furniture, to apologize, to buy Szafransky a suit of clothes and resurrect him – give him and Delman a job on the floor. To be twenty years old and still not have the answer to anything, to have no one to turn to except the Negro at your side whom you respect and fear, and who, you suspect, hates your guts. The whole world was winking behind his back.

He took a last look around. The deputy was standing near the children, pouring them cereal as they sprawled on the floor in front of the TV.

'We're going,' said Judd.

'Checked the list?' he asked.

'Don't need to,' said Delman. 'Everything's ours except the appliances. Just need your initials, since the man cut out.'

'Then you've done your damage. So why not get the hell out? I'll sign your paper and then I'll personally chase off the first one of you that ever tries to enter this house again.'

Delman liked driving a full truck: the skill it required, the drag of something behind him – he especially liked being an obstacle on the inclines, grinding up the hills at ten miles an hour. He would have preferred doing it alone. He liked talking to himself, and now he had Junior in the cab and the boss's big ear and the boss's piece of tail hooked into his warehouse.

'Oooo-eeee, I tell you,' he suddenly burst out, and if he had been alone he would have left it there, but with Junior he had to finish it. 'That was something else.'

Junior looked mad. Said nothing, held a book but wasn't reading.

'You pissed off at something?'

'Just thinking.'

'Want a beer?'

'I said I was just thinking.'

'Just thinking,' he repeated, tapping his forehead. 'Give yourself a headache, all that thinking,' he shouted over the racket. A metal racket of an ancient engine straining against a governor, the uninsulated hood, the shaking, whining, ungreased metal. 'You're on a vacation, man,' he yelled. 'You're going to Europe in four-five months, and you got a set-up going here that's always going to keep you in bread, and you're only twenty years old, man. What the hell you always thinking all the time for?'

And you're a white boy, Junior. Your old man picks up five hundred on a bad day, five thousand on a good one. I've seen him sell ten thousand dollars on a single afternoon. When Delman thought too hard of the boss and Junior, he thought of the Czar and all the little Czareviches, how they must have worried too. Always worrying about where to go and how to spend it. Then: *plunk-plunk-plunk*. Delman's fantasies hovered between being a Cossack and being a revolutionary soldier. He was in the Red Army today, no doubt about it, with his heart in the basement of Malick's Furniture or, better yet, in the warehouse where he'd made a room of his own for lunch and dinner. Father and Son, hands on paddle, kneeling. And for Mrs Simmons – What? There must have been times when nothing was slow and ugly enough.

'What's that you're reading?'

Over the whining and clatter of gears, Judd began to speak, then to shout: 'It's not what I'm reading. It's not just a single book. Reading this book is like going to the Szafranskys' day after day – are you listening. Delman? Can you hear me over the motor? It's like confronting something purer than your own situation, you know? This book happens in Paris fifty years ago, but it's today, it's me, it's you. Delman, listen: Haven't you ever seen something so close that it frightened you – or disgusted you? So much so that you had to turn away from it, thankful that it wasn't your situation? Haven't you ever felt that at last you've seen something *final*, the end of something, some definitive corruption, only to return to your own little world and see that it's just slightly less pure, less corrupt, less crystalline? Only slightly? Haven't you? That's how I feel about myself and about the store. That's how I feel about hose poor fucking people we took the furniture from. As though everything that I can understand is radiating out from this little book, embracing more and more things that I can't understand, and I want to look away from all of it. Delman' – and now he was shouting, slapping the dashboard so that Delman would at least look his way and quit smirking for just a second – 'I feel like it's drowning me. I feel like we've all died a little bit today. Delman, do you understand?'

77

Dunkelblau

Willi Nadeau has lain abed since birth, dumb and apparently unreachable, his bones as fragile as rods of hollow glass. He sleeps on pillows, his crib is padded. He is four. His mother is forty-two and has lost her only family. The boy, the lump, is all she lives for. Two succeeding pregnancies have ended in the seventh month. She remembers a burning, the heavy settling, and knows she is carrying another death. A brother is stillborn and a sister, lumpish as Willi, survives three months. Willi lives – if that's the word – because he is the first, before she developed antibodies to his father. His parents are profoundly incompatible.

In 1944, Army research synthesizes a thyroid extract. The pills are tiny, mottled brown. Two weeks after giving him the medicine, his mother feels his neck twitch as she sponges him in the kitchen sink. A week later, he kicks, and in a moment as dramatic in his family as Helen Keller at the water pump, he starts singing the words and music of 'Don't Fence Me In'. He justifies all her faith in keeping him at home, in reading the medical journals and pestering doctors, the four years of talking to him in both her languages, reading to him, hanging maps and showing pictures.

Like many a genius before him, though he is nearly five, he speaks in complete sentences before taking his first step. He demands his dozen glasses of cold milk a day be served in a heated bunny mug. He is a wilful, confident child, his mother's image. He likes the feel of heat on his lips, the icy cold going down. Each glass has to have a spoonful of molasses or of Horlick's Malted Milk, unstirred, at the bottom. No flecks of cream can show. The nightly slabs of liver or other organ meats, purchased on special rations, are shaped into states or countries, predetermined by Willi and his mother from prior consultation. She starts taking him to Carnegie Library and Museum as soon as he can walk.

He memorizes the Pittsburgh trolley-numbering system. The Holy Roman Emperors, the Popes, the Kings of England. He memorizes everything, his brain is ruthlessly absorptive, a sponge, like his bones and muscles. Toy-sized yellow and red trolleys pass across a forested valley outside his bedroom window. He is still unsteady on his feet in the winter of 1945 when they take their number 10 trolley down to Liberty Avenue and then one of the 70s out to Oakland to the Library and Museum.

His first memories are of the Library, the smell of old books, the low chairs and tables of the children's room, and of staring into the adult reading room – no children allowed – while his mother checks the carts of new arrivals. The adult room is a cave of wonders, where steam rises from the piled-up coats and scarves. The six-storey ceiling, the polished wood and the corridors of books overhead absorb the coughs and page-shufflings of the white-haired men and women who sit around the tables. That is the world that awaits him – admission to the adult room, permission to sit under those long-necked lamps that hang from the rafters six floors up to nearly graze the tabletops, flooding the tables with a rich yellow light under bright green shades. It is a world worth waiting for, like the dark blue volumes of *My Book House* which his mother reads from every night and which are laid out above his bed, mint green to marine blue, a band of promise to take him from infancy to adolescence.

The main hall that connects the Library with the Museum is lined with paintings that his mother holds him up to see. Murky oils, Pittsburgh scenes from the Gilded Age, operagoers alighting from horse-drawn cabs in the gaslit snows of Grant Street, children riding their high-wheeled bicycles down Center Avenue. He feels the stab of every passing, irretrievable image. He can look in those faces of 1870, at the girls with their hands in fur muffs and their collars up, their eyes glittering and cheeks round and pink and full of life, and know exactly what his mother is thinking, because she is always thinking it: even these happy children are all gone, as dead as the snows and horses and all but the finest buildings, gone forever.

And there are darker Pittsburgh landscapes, with the orange glow of hellish pits fanning through the falling snow, the play of fires lighting the genteel ridges high above. Pittsburgh, with its blackened skies and acrid fumes, its intimate verticality of heaven and hell, forces allegory on all who live there. 'So simplistic,' she says, drawing his finger so close to the canvas that the guards stand and snap their fingers. Columned mansions on gaslit streets, perched above the unbanked fires, the bright pouring of molten streams of steel by sooty, sweating men far below. Heaven and Hell on the Monongahela. On their trolley rides, high on the sides of smoke-blackened buildings, he sees faded signs in lettering he can't read but knows is old. That the signs have accidentally survived but mean nothing fills him with dread and wonder, and he asks if the companies are still there, *Isidor Ash, Iron-Monger.* Those three and four-digit telephone numbers, do they still work, who do you get if you call, an imprisoned voice? Where do they all go?

He thinks of Hans von Kaltenborn and Gabriel Heatter and all the singers as being inside the radio. He presses his forehead against the back of the radio, inhaling the hot electric thrill of music from faraway cities, watching for miniature Jack Bennys and Edgar Bergens. 'Be very quiet, and quick, they'll run if they see you,' his mother says. In 1945, his father calls all the men on the street over to study the first sketches of the 1946 Ford, with headlights in the fenders and no running boards. When the war is finally over he promises to junk their '38 Packard for one of these streamlined babies.

Nineteen forty-five means the children gather at the top of the dead-end street to intercept their fathers as they turn in, to be swept to their driveways like young footmen standing on the running boards and clinging to the mirrors and spotlights. The loudest kids live across the street. They're the three sons of the football coach at Duquesne. In the winter, he sleds with his father, held tight in his lap while two of the coach's sons stand on a toboggan and pass them, arguing about the war. We'll win because the Russians are on our side and Russians are eight feet tall.

In the winter, his mother piles up old papers and boards around the edge of their five-by-five porch off the kitchen and floods it in order to teach him ice-skating. She ties a pillow around him and lets him walk around the edges of the porch. His feet and ankles are undefined, like pillows. Coming down hard on an ankle, a hip, an arm, can crack a bone. But his father is Canadian and his parents met there and they skated and skied together before he was born. Knowing how to skate makes him a better son. It is important to his father and to his doctor for him to pass for normal as soon as possible.

They live on a crowded street at the edge of a heavily wooded valley that surrounds a tributary of the Allegheny River. In the winter, his father and the football coach ski down a path they have cleared to the rocks and boulders that mark the stream-bed. He's older than the coach, but a better skier and skater. 'What a beautiful animal your father is,' his mother says, watching him from the porch. On clear winter days, a rarity in Pittsburgh in those years, he can see through the blackened branches to the top of the Gulf Building and red lights on Mt. Washington. Willi transplants all his mother's night-time readings of Robin Hood into those woods. It is Sherwood Forest. Pittsburgh is Nottingham. The deer and bear and Merry Men are all out there, somewhere.

In the spring, when the ice is a morning's whitened blister over the concrete, the porch becomes his mother's studio. The buds have not yet opened, yet she arranges her paints and papers on the card table and carries out a chair to do her watercolours. She puts Mozart records on to play and keeps the kitchen door open so she can hear.

She brought her paints and bundles of drawings from Europe. Everything else is lost. Her brushes burst with colours that never drip. It reminds the boy of Disney cartoons, when a full paintbrush washes over the screen, creating the world as it touches down. That's how her paintings grow. Her colours seem especially intense, and have German names which never have satisfactory equivalents in English. He doesn't know they're enemy words; he thinks of them as irreplaceable tablets of pure colour. He laughs at *dunkelblau,* a funny word that becomes a code between them. Sometimes a fat man is Herr Dunkelblau. The last volumes of *My Book House* where the stories require too much explaining, are deep blue, dunkelblau. Other times she lies in bed behind closed window shades, holding her head with a dunkelblau. The opposite of dark, *dunkel,* he knows is *hell,* light.

'Watercolour must come down like rain,' she says. 'It should come quick like a shower and make everything shine, like rain. But it should not touch everything, not like oils.' Oils sound old and dutiful, like the museum.

'A paintstorm,' he says.

She sets him up with his paper and brushes and Woolworth's paints though he sometimes sneaks a swipe of her colours, thick and gripping as mud on his brush. Every few minutes she has to blow soot off her paper. When her German paints are gone, she'll quit painting.

She's a woman of Old World habits. Mondays and Fridays she does the wash. Because of the soot she has to take down all the white curtains, beat the rugs and bedspreads, take off the slipcovers and scrub the white shirts whose collars come back each day so black they look dipped in ink. Tuesdays are dyeing days, mixing the boxes of Rit that line the window ledge over the washtubs, to bring lime green to a Pittsburgh winter, or dunkelblau to a hot summer. Thursdays she makes the soap. Antiseptic odours fill the house, making his eyes run. Orange cakes of fresh soap are cut into shapes of states and countries. The shirts and sheets sink into the hot tub where she adds broken cakes of soap, and he adds the drops of blueing, and loses himself in the smoky trail of its dispersion. Such excitement for a child, catching the world in one of its paradoxes: adding stains to make clothes whiter. He can watch it spread forever, like watching cigarette smoke rise from his mother's ashtray or from the stubs his father burns down to nothingness, the smoke going straight up then suddenly hitting an invisible barrier and spreading out. On cleaning days, he's allowed to play in the coal bin, reading the old marks and dates of deliveries from before he was born, and throw his clothes in at the last minute, standing against the cold enamel of the washing tub as the islands of his shirt and pants and underwear resist, then drown.

Wednesdays she does the shopping, which means an afternoon of baking bread and an evening of stirring the bright orange colour tabs into the margarine. It's another low-grade art experience, like the blueing, with the added pleasure of being able to eat some of the results, melted over a bowl of Puffed Rice.

In the late summer of 1945, the war in Europe is over and the spirit on the radio is always upbeat. The arrival of troop ships is announced and train schedules from New York or Los Angeles tell Pittsburghers where to meet their boys. His mother listens for news of Europe, but there's never enough. Nineteen forty-five is a year to gladden everyone but her. 'Just because you're German and you lost?' he asks her once, remembering the taunt of the coach's sons, and she runs from the room. He asks her who the best singer is – Bing Crosby, she says – and the funniest person – Bob Hope, she guesses, though they both prefer Jack Benny –

and the prettiest woman – she couldn't say, ladies don't know who's pretty that way, but maybe he could ask his father – so, okay, the handsomest man – Van Johnson, they say – but the men she thinks are handsomer aren't around any more.

Nineteen forty-five is the happiest year in his father's life and in the lives of the men on their street, whose jobs will all be getting bigger. There'll be houses to buy and new businesses to open and of course new cars, especially new cars. They're all thinking of leaving Pittsburgh. The Depression mentality is over, they've won the war, they're Number One in the world. But everything about 1945 makes his mother sadder, especially everyone's happiness. She shows him pictures of old men and women and children in striped pyjamas. 'So now we know that men are hideous beasts,' she says. 'What kind of world is this?' Nineteen forty-five is the saddest year in existence. His father says it's like a sickness, her questions. You're crazy, he says. We'll all be rich if she'll just shut up and give him a chance.

She's busier than ever on the afternoons when the housework and shopping are done, painting the full, dark green summer of August, 1945. The atom bomb ends the war with Japan. He watches the woods and asks her if that isn't a bit of smoke rising through the trees, coming from the bottom of the woods, along the riverbank.

His father's winter ski-run offers a sightline through the woods if he goes between their house and Hutchisons' and stretches out on his stomach and peers down it as far as he can. He sees nothing at first, just the collapse of the vanishing point into a thicket of trees, but then he sees something: men, and maybe a horse. Horses in the woods! The woods are uninhabited, vast and practically virgin timber. When he shouts 'Men!' and 'Horses!' his mother says, 'Oh, God!' and puts her brush in a glass of clean water.

They go out the front of the house, to the top of the street. They walk down a block, turn and come to another dead-end street much like theirs, but poorer. The houses are low and wooden, more like sheds or garages. Their house is brick. Dogs and chickens run over the yards. Where the street abuts on a different part of the woods, a rutted path eases down into the dark. From there, they can see what the forest has given birth to: many men and some children, and two horses pulling a wagon.

'Gypsies!' she whispers.

Already the women on the street are chasing down their dogs and loose chickens. They stand at the top of the trail and shout at the wagoners in words he can't understand. 'It's Polish,' his mother says. 'They're warning them not to come too close.' Children come out of the houses, carrying utensils and beating them with spoons.

'Stay close,' she says.

They wait for the wagon to mount the hill. The wagon is fat, ready to split, decked out in bells and leather straps with metal pots hanging from the corners. The men wear black hats with silver discs around the brims. There are no women. There are boys with long curly hair under their hats and men with open shirts and blackened arms beating spoons against the pots making a kind of chant. Street dogs are howling. The gypsies stop the noise just in front of the line of Polish women, and the boys lower the cart's back gate to expose a stone wheel operated by an old, white-haired man. The man wears an earring, something the boy has never seen, and it frightens him.

She wants him to watch. She holds him up, as she does in front of the paintings at the Library. And then she walks the length of the wagon with him, peering inside. 'You should see and not be frightened,' she says. The gypsies don't seem to care. The gypsy children follow them, laughing, and pull at his mother's skirt.

'Stop it!' she commands. 'You're very ill-behaved.'

They pull again.

'Brats! *Bengeln!*'

They giggle louder. *'Unverschämt!'*

When she speaks harshly like that, she's usually very angry and usually the person she's angry with, his father, does not understand. Bad behaviour is the only thing that gets her angry. Other things make her sad. Finally one of the men inside the wagon barks out a command and the children back off.

'Come to my street when you finish,' she says, pointing over the row of low, unpainted houses. 'I have some things.' The Polish women are now lined up with knives and scissors and some large cooking pots.

In one of the dark blue *Book Houses* there's a picture of a gypsy man holding a white horse in the moonlight, calling under a girl's window. For Willi, gypsies are a people out of the dream world of pictures and legends, and this is the first time he's seen something from his books come alive. In his light green world of *Book House* the pictures are all of talking animals. Later on they become magicians in tall caps decorated with stars and moons, then knights on horseback, Crusaders and explorers. He's not given up the notion that their woods contain Robin Hood and his men, and now that it's given birth to gypsies, he takes heart again.

They hurry back to their house and his mother empties all the kitchen drawers and takes out the pots and pans and cake dishes, everything metal that is scratched or dented or has grown dull. She bundles them in a sheet and lays them on the front lawn. Then she grabs her drawing pad and some pencils and starts sketching from the front of the house. It's the first time she's sketched the street and not the woods. The beauty, she says, is all in the back.

In the front are houses just like theirs, and an open lot across the street where the larger boys play football and fathers play catch with their sons. He can't play – any shock can still shatter his bones. The opposite side of the street is much higher than theirs, even the empty lot is higher than the roof of their house. He can stand on the grass and see over his house and over the woods all the way to the Gulf Building. In other summers the sons of the football coach batted tennis balls and scuffed-up golf balls into high arcs over his house and the Hutchisons' into the trees and valley beyond.

Before the gypsies turn the corner, with the distant banging of the pots and clanging of the bells, and then the sharp cracking of the horse-whip, his mother has sketched in the roof lines, the trees and the open lot. She's gotten the big tricycles in the driveways and one parked car.

'Gypsies! Lock your houses, take in your children, mind your dogs!' women on the street yell out, but soon enough they stand in their driveways clutching their knives and cooking pots. His mother pulls the covering sheet off her pile of metal utensils and tells a man everything needs polishing and sharpening and smoothing out, and she doesn't care how long it takes. By the time they're finished, she's gotten their picture, every detail in place with her pencils and charcoal: the horses, the children in their hats chasing dogs, all the clutter the wagon contains. She keeps sharpening her pencils against a block of sandpaper. She ignores the children who watch over her shoulder. Normally she stops anything she's drawing in order to demonstrate. When they leave, her arms are shaking, her hair is sticking to her forehead.

Later, when she sprays fixative, she says she hasn't worked so hard since her days at art school. She adds the drawing to her oldest sketches, those of German cathedral doors and Egyptian pottery and Nefertiti's head from the Berlin Museum, and country scenes of cows and horses and farmers bundling hay.

'A drawing should show everything,' she says, and that's what she likes about the gypsies; they are art, frightening and fascinating, their wagons are beautiful because they totally express the lives they lead.

'The war was fought over people like them,' she says. 'And people like us.'

But the gypsies don't go away. Smoke from their encampment drifts up from the riverside, settles in a blue haze with the rest of Pittsburgh's smog. Through the early fall they're a familiar sight on the streets, and gradually the girls and women appear too, dressed in bandannas and wide colourful skirts. They come to the front doors, bold as you please, the neighbours say, offering to do housework and tell fortunes, selling eggs and strange-smelling flowers so strong they can drug you in the night. His mother draws the line at letting gypsies in the house. She doubts the wide skirts are purely a fashion statement.

As the leaves turn and drop they can see through to the encampment. There are four wagons and several cooking fires. His mother sketches it all, the ghostly outlines of the wagons through the tracery of branches, the horses, the pen for animals rumoured but unseen – bears, panthers, half-tamed wolves. It's a curious relationship she has with gypsies, to admire but not to trust, to adore as subjects while wishing they'd leave. The boy wants them gone. They excite his mother and make her strange. The gypsies are closer than he'd thought possible. He can hear them at night.

The assault begins with the coach's sons. They throw crushed lime-stones from the open lot across the street. They bat stones and golf balls, they use slingshots and their well-trained arms. They sneak down the slope and throw from the Nadeaus' side of the street, even from the corridor between their house and the Hutchisons', until his mother chases them off. From the sharp whinny of the horses, the barking and the occasional echo of stones on wood or metal, he knows the stones are striking home.

In early November the gypsies leave. 'West Virginia,' people say, a proper place for gypsies. Winter comes and the snows. His father and the coach are back on their ski run and the boy is strong enough to skate across the flooded porch. His father's plans are to leave Sears and go south, now that the country is back to normal. No more Carnegie Library, no more streetcar numbers to memorize, and maybe he'll never get a card for the adult reading room. When his father mentions the word 'south' his mother shudders and leaves the room.

Being European, she doesn't believe in baby-sitters. She doesn't leave him until he is strong enough to walk on his own and be careful with appliances. On New Year's Eve they're invited to a party next door at Hutch and Marge's, friends of his father, a gregarious man. It's a cold, snowless night and he's allowed to sleep in the living room on the sofa with the radio on to see if he can stay awake for 1946. His mother promises she'll come over and wake him.

The Christmas tree is up, the electric train circles the wrinkled sheet city of snowy hills. When he wakes up with only the tree lights on, the radio is humming but not playing music and he thinks he must have slept through everything. Nineteen forty-five is the first year of his consciousness, the year of his true birth, and now it is over. It has died, and he is born. The worst year in history, his mother says. The best, his father counters. He gets up and looks next door to Hutch and Marge's where a light is on and it looks close enough to run to, barefoot in his pyjamas.

The door is open and the vestibule is jammed with fur coats. The air inside is hot and thick with smoke and forced, loud laughter. His father and the coach are the oldest men in the room, and the loudest and happiest. Theirs is a young street of mainly childless couples ready now to start their families. The women are getting pregnant, there's a sharp bite of sexuality in the air, lives are going places but still on hold, the country is going places, big places, but hasn't quite gotten over its wartime gloom and pinchpenny habits. Those are the attitudes he hears and takes as truth. He sides with his father in the arguments because his father's a great one for looking ahead, on the bright side, to the future.

The aluminum Train of Tomorrow is barrelling down the tracks, taking them all to a chrome-plated, streamlined, lightweight future and cities like Pittsburgh with their dirty bricks and labour problems are in the way of progress. If you're in the way, better clear out. A damned shame some people just can't get in the spirit.

'And you think the south is progress?' his mother demands.

His father is singing, with his back to the fireplace. Not French songs, the way they usually ask him to at parties, but Bing Crosby songs. Around the mirror over the mantel, Hutch and Marge have pasted all their Christmas cards. Their tree is bigger than the Nadeaus', and the lights blink and some other candles bubble. Everyone is outlined in blue and red and faint ghostly yellow. All the women except his mother are blondes, with big round coral earrings and bright lipstick that stains their cigarettes. Some still wear little hats with their veils half pulled down.

He stands in the hallway, leaning against a fur coat, peering around the edge. They're singing the New Year's Song his mother taught him, and they're blowing on paper trumpets and strapping on little cone-shaped hats. His mother stands at the far end of the living room, by the kitchen door where the light is strongest. *I don't feel like celebrating,* she declared earlier and his father had left on his own, shouting, *You can't ruin it for me,* but she went anyway, a few minutes later. He peels off his pyjamas and wraps himself in her fur coat. No one notices him. Her head is down and her hands hold the sides of her face, pressing down her veil. She seems to be rocking back and forth. Someone has set a lime-green party hat on top of her black pillbox with the single pheasant feather.

They're counting backwards. When the numbers get smaller, the noise increases and he's shouting with everyone, trailing the heavy coat, 'It's 1946! It's 1946!' running naked into the living room like the Baby New Year with the sash. A few women hug him and squeeze him tight in their unsteadiness. His father looks around to see how he's gotten there – he has Marge and another woman on his arms – and all the men are going around collecting kisses.

'For God's sake, Liesl –' his father calls and she drops to her knees with her arms open as he pushes his way to her through a jitterbugging dance floor. It seems to take hours. She rolls up her veil to touch her eyes with a paper napkin.

Her fur coat falls from his shoulders as she lifts him. He rubs his cheek against the rough and the fine mesh of her veil, feels her cool satin dress against his naked body, and they dance. It seems the whirling will go on forever, even as the music dies out, then the laughter, and he and his mother dance their way out the door, shivering, across the icy grass to home.

Snake in Flight over Pittsburgh

Two young men – boys, really – are playing chess in a living room in Pittsburgh in the late summer of 1960. Their shoes are polished, they wear flannel pants with white suspenders, formal shirts with pearl studs, maroon bowties and cummerbunds. Their jackets are on the sofa. They are eighteen, home from their first year of college. Terry has gone from high school honours to Princeton honours. Alex has struggled through the year at Oberlin. Nothing serious; just a confirmation that absolutes do exist in the world, and Terry, who plays better chess and who'd gotten better grades and who goes to a more competitive school is by all accounts smarter than Alex.

Before a spurt of growth that cleared his skin and lifted him to well over six feet, Terry was a pimply, bulb-headed boy with an air of incipient officiousness. Alex, who was then much taller, hasn't grown since: he's average, but beginning to fade. Already his hair-parting is suspiciously wide, and a bay has opened between his temple and forehead to receive it. He can still easily hide a tiny tonsure that marks the confluence of the combed latitudes over the vault of his skull and the thick, brushed longitudes down the back. Soon, he'll look like Adlai Stevenson. Europe, he calls his widening forehead, mowing down the jungles behind. He is particularly aware of his bald spot when Francesca stands behind him as he crouches over the chess board, not that she's likely to, today.

Ironically, they met in an eighth-grade moment of shared equality. In high school, Terry got only two A's. One was in English, the other in German. Alex also managed just two A's, in the same two courses. In their intensely competitive school, however, every letter grade was sliced three ways – plus, plain and minus – and every other grade of Terry's was A+. Most of Alex's were A– (a particularly apt, almost evocative judgement, he's come to feel) when not B+ (the cruellest mark of all), or even a solid B. He considers himself at best an A– person in a B– world. Terry is something else, entirely.

Alex is in love with the whole concept of Terry Franklin's family: his being, his house, his parents, his relatives, his younger brothers and especially, his twin sister. They favour simple things, quality goods bought in cash, when not home-made. Terry's chess set is home-made, something fashioned in a Scoutish summer out of clothespins. What a marvellous thing it is, to Alex's mind, not to lose things, to be living in the only house you've ever known, to have parents at home, and to fashion bishops, rooks and knights from simple tacks, nails and various screws. The king wears an eye-hook. Terry has ridden that modest set to the big leagues of amateur chess in Western Pennsylvania – a 2200 ranking from the USCF. Alex thinks of that chess set as somehow the proof of true talent, the phenom's arrival with patched shoes and a slab of leather who shames the American Legion boys in their flannel suits with twenty-dollar Spaldings and bevelled cleats.

There are rumours of lineage, of a remote ancestor from Philadelphia, perhaps not quite legitimate. In the nineteenth century a certain Benj Franklin crossed the Alleghenies and established the family on vast tracts south of the present city. His mother's family, mountaineers and moonshiners, according to more legend, had been in the hills since the Revolution. Both sides have been there ever since.

Terry's parents, Alex is convinced, lie at the heart of their son's achievement, which is another way of saying *his* parents are to blame for his relative mediocrity. Dr Franklin, a research chemist at Westinghouse, is older than most fathers. He'd established himself in the world before getting married. Terry does not remember him other than grey and bald, yet he has never bested his father in any competition. Dr Franklin still drives the lane against Terry's guarding, still sinks his free-throws twenty in a row, still sculls on weekends as he did forty years ago at MIT. He heads a nature group, publishes a bird-watchers' letter, advises the Scouts, and chairs the local Republican committee. He's a senior in the United Presbyterian Church, and still, he reads. Greek and Latin. The classic novels, the latest biographies, histories. The house is full of books, none of them in paperback.

Of course, Alex exempts Dr Franklin from *too* much knowledge, or *too* proper an attitude. Alex has gone on a demonstration against segregated housing in Cleveland, and he's attended a couple of meetings of a local SNCC chapter. He's heard enough around the Franklin table over the years to know what the family believes: people prefer to live and to travel with their own kind, though Alex's activism is tolerated, even respected, in an amused sort of way. Actually, he was grandstanding just a bit when he told them about the demonstrations. He hadn't gone on the Greyhound trip to Memphis and Nashville. And he had left the picket line in Cleveland before the police broke it up.

He was trying to impress Francesca. She was eating at home that night, a rare event, and not with her boyfriend. Alex looks on each night he is at the Franklins' – which is most nights – as his last chance to save her. His last chance at personal happiness. Any day now, his future will open before him, and he'll stumble into a profession or a set of attitudes, something as simple for others but impossible for him as a distinctive haircut or clothing style or political attitude that will reflect or perhaps define the man he senses within him.

Alex has often wondered what, exactly, accounts for their friendship. He is grateful for it – without it, he might have died – but he never quite understood it. He and Terry have nothing in common. If he has sympathies, they are with the arts, with chaos, destruction. If he has ruling passions, they are bitterness and resentment and monstrous self-pity.

On the day he met Terry, all the eighth-graders had written personal essays entitled 'My Typical Day'. His was slightly lurid – he was a natural exaggerator – and the teacher went out of her way to praise it. Alex and his family were new to Pittsburgh, the latest stop in their gypsy existence. He'd exaggerated that as well. His parents had started a furniture store in a squalid satellite town, one of those cinders in space that never quite became a suburb, and they were at it eighteen hours a day, freeing Alex for sleeping and rising, meals and entertainment, entirely on his own. He was an only child who went to movies alone on week-nights, stayed up late for Jack Paar, and exercised greasy options for dinner each night, mindless of milk and vegetables.

He sees now what Terry was driving at. How vulnerable he is to the charms Terry can offer. They live in a world of mutual envy, a Mexican stand-off of incredulity.

Alex resents anything that separates him from communion with the Franklins. He resents being shorter and slower and less co-ordinated, less intelligent and clean-featured, less noble and religious, less hard-working and clearly committed, less universally admired, less socketed in the community. He resents the smells of his parents' apartment, the stale, bluish air, and having parents – nobodies from nowhere – who smoke and leave their bottles around the house, who wouldn't mind if he smoked and drank, and give him no credit for choosing not to, who've failed so miserably in so many undertakings.

The Franklins go back at least five generations in Pittsburgh, and none of them, apparently, has known a Pittsburgh life of millwork, squalor, black-lung, or Catholicism. Hardly any of the aunts and uncles and sturdy, reliable cousins that Alex has come to know by the dozens in the past five years, smoke, drink, or even swear.

Alex has suffered through a bad freshman year at Oberlin. The only girls he's dated have been civil rights activists who encourage his liberalism – given his wretched class origins he's something of an aberration – but who duck into Cleveland for weekends to test their 'existential commitment' with black men in the ghetto. He's awash in self-pity, fearing himself short-changed in the manhood department. Terry suggests they're just the wrong girls for him.

'You know who's right for you, don't you? Francesca? She's been after me for years about you.'

Terry found a girl at Vassar who's visited him twice this summer in Pittsburgh, when the tennis tour makes it convenient. She's on the Vassar freshman team, nationally ranked, a Davis Cup prospect. She can give Terry more than a good game. Terry won their club's junior championship; he's not accustomed to losing anything, and he doesn't make an especially appealing spectacle of himself, whaling away from the baseline against Susan Stanbury's powerful returns. Alex, with club privileges, has a standing invitation to swim or play. He has never held a racquet. His parents have never belonged to anything that requires a vote.

She's on tour today, and can't be here for the wedding. It may cause a break-up, though Terry's too well-mannered to deliver ultimatums. Susan is a small blond girl with chopped-off hair and a pug nose. She favours pearls, but smells of chlorine. Alex doesn't credit her with much sexuality or any charm – her whole conversation consists of tennis terms and tour dates and pointers for Terry's game – though at least she'd not sneak off to ghetto hotels to test her commitment. Her father is an investment banker in New York. Terry visited her there in the winter and has been taken to dinner at the Princeton Club. It is hard for Alex even to imagine his Pittsburgh friend, accomplished as he is, a boy of undoubted genius who'd been too busy to date in high school, whose family ties are so strong he's never eaten in a restaurant, never spent money at a movie or at a sporting contest, never been a fan – only a participant – actually *finding* a girl and apparently knowing what to do with her and how to keep it going over a Pittsburgh summer, which can blight nearly anything.

He resents the way the Franklins embrace the girl, how Francesca takes her downtown on the assumption that a couple of dates with her brother and a visit will result in a marriage and move to Pittsburgh. 'We'll be sisters!' she cried, a stomach-turning proposal, thinks Alex. She can say goodbye to Saks Fifth Avenue and Lord & Taylor and say hello to Kaufman's and Joseph Horne's. Pittsburgh at least had a Gimbel's which can take her credit card.

'How marvellous you're a Presbyterian, too!' Mrs Franklin had observed. 'I didn't think there *were* any in New York City.'

Alex has loved Francesca since the day in the eighth grade, after his first dinner at their house. He'd been impressed and a little frightened by the elaborate 'grace' participated in by all. They held hands under the table. He was seated between the twins and hadn't known Terry was, as it were, duplicated (they looked nothing alike, nor were their accomplishments in any way similar). Francesca had missed a year due to a childhood illness; she was the tallest and prettiest seventh-grader in the school.

He was sure she'd forget him, but the next day at school she called out, 'Hi, Alex', and stood by his locker as he loaded books and forgot what he needed, forgot where he was going. She walked with him down the corridor, carrying her books in a young girl's swaying manner, against an emerging bosom. She cocked her head to hear him better though he had nothing to say and they were the same height anyway. People had seen them together, that's what mattered, and they didn't look, he felt, implausible.

That had been his moment. He knew five years ago she was going to be beautiful (but never *this* beautiful, so much beauty he couldn't look on her), and more: kind, intelligent without arrogance.

'She asked about you,' Terry would say. 'Always asks me, when's Alex going to ask me out?'

'Oh, sure,' he'd say, usually over chess.

'She says she thinks about you all the time.'

'Oh, for Christ's sake, Terry. What makes you think I care what she thinks?'

'Think how convenient it would be,' he'd say, back in the ninth and tenth grades. 'There's her room, there's an extra bed up here ... in the middle of the night, who would know?'

'Just cut it out, okay?'

'Is that a blush I see?'.

She still wasn't taken, back then. She'd have a date or two but nothing serious. Francesca, genetically incapable of imperfection, achieved a quality altogether different from Terry's. She has height, fair hair, and a model's high-planed features. She has Terry's intelligence but not his ambition. She has warmth and humour, a suppressed laughter that Alex can feel just by looking at her, as though together (he fantasizes) they are sharing a joke at the world. She has open sympathies with liberal causes.

Just last month after dinner, she came downstairs, dressed to go out with her boyfriend, the one she'd gotten serious about while Alex was away at Oberlin. The boyfriend was more than that; they all called him, facetiously, he hoped, her fiancé. He was a college senior, a threat Alex had to take seriously. A Harvard senior, with many attributes that come easily to Harvard men, like a sportscar and easy manners and helpful contacts in the business world through his father, who was, like Susan Stanbury's father, an investment banker.

As Francesca was coming downstairs, Terry met her halfway up and gave her breast a noticeable jiggle and pinch, something that caused her to frown and push away.

Her father was at the base of the stairs. 'Problem, honey?'

'Just him.'

'Terry? You have something to say to your sister?'

Francesca pulled a little at her sweater.

'I told my sister she was looking very nice for her young man,' Terry replied. 'She must have misunderstood. I'll have to learn to speak more clearly.'

'I think so, too,' said Dr Franklin. 'What do you think, Alex?'

He was afraid at that moment of saying too much, of emptying all the grief in his heart and reducing the nature of his relationship with that marvellous family to a sham. In a word or two he might have acknowledged all that Terry suspected of his motives and held implicitly over him. He merely shrugged and muttered, 'Okay, I guess.'

'That's all, Alex? Only okay?' She sounded hurt. Then came that suppressed little laugh as she pointed a finger at Terry. '"If you like that sort of thing,"' she said in a mocking voice, 'is that it? Just an ugly sister who gets in the way and doesn't play chess and doesn't like some of the other games her brother plays – okay for someone like that, is that it?'

And by then she was at the base of the stairs with her father and Alex. Terry had gone up to his lab. 'Alex is right, daddy.' She picked up on a dinner conversation. She was folding a pastel scarf to tie over her hair, a sign that she and her Harvard boy were going driving. 'I'd vote for Kennedy, too, if I were old enough.'

'Oh, heaven forbid!' her father gasped with a theatrical groan. 'Sharper than a serpent's tooth.'

She stood on the porch waiting for her date. Alex was suddenly alone downstairs. He could have gone out to the porch and stood with her – she would have liked that, it might even have appeared a little gallant, plausible, to neighbours. He yearned to join her, a last chance to stop the future, even for the sweet pain of turning her over to her Harvard Buzz. He could do it, he thought, even at this late hour, say the things and make them count. Reveal his secret identity. Show her that it had been *his* love, all these years, not her father, not the church, not the ghastly Buzz, that maintained her, kept her safe, kept her whole. Kept her brother from her. *He* was the engine that drove the Franklin family, the heat, the light. He could make her know it, now. But he hated the way it would look. He wasn't a bird-dog.

'Alex,' Dr Franklin turned midway up the stairs. 'I don't think your father got as good a deal as he hoped. You might ask him about it.' Then he was gone, up to his study to work on his Latin, to read his Bible, and eventually to join his wife in sleep. Terry was working. Francesca waited.

The needle Dr Franklin had just inserted was more painful to him than the thought of Buzz blaring the horn of his Belvedere just outside.

Dr Franklin, in his methodical way, had discovered that Alex's father cheated him badly. What he perhaps didn't know was that the cheating was deliberate. When his parents started their store, Alex's role had been to enlist his friends' support. 'See that all your rich friends get the word,' his father had said. 'Tell them they'll get the deal of a lifetime.' The Franklins had come around late, but they'd finally come, cash in hand, for three bedrooms' worth. A few weeks after the sale he'd heard his mother shouting, 'How *could* you? That's despicable!'

His father was silent, as usual.

'*Borax!*' she cried.

'So? I'm Borax. I know what I am. You see jerks, you take them for a ride. You make your breaks in this world. You don't mind spending it, so don't complain about how you get it. You think maybe this jerk'll give us a break on a Westinghouse refrigerator? Well, I got news for you. It don't work that way. Nobody gets a break.'

Alex had determined that night, listening to them fight, that he would hate his father and the business he was in and the world that had created him, and he would pray for its failure and destruction, in the name of the Franklins and all the others he'd been forced to defraud. Worse than anything, it was the bed that Francesca slept on, and the dresser she stored her sweaters in, the nightstand and lamp she read by, the desk she did her work on, that they had sold the Franklins.

Today might be the saddest day of Alex's life. Upstairs, Francesca is preparing herself for sacrifice. She's graduated from high school and turned down her scholarship to Bryn Mawr in order to marry Buzz Howarth, her Harvard boy. His father is buying them a 'cottage' – his word – in Cambridge. Francesca will keep house a year, start a family – she's anxious for that, according to Terry – then maybe when Rod (his real name, a word so pulsatingly ugly, so grotesquely appropriate, that Alex can barely utter it) starts the B-School, she'll go to B.U. or Tufts, at night. She's eighteen. She'll never see college, never date, never hear from other men anything of her exquisiteness.

She's been seen and claimed by a college man whose family doesn't cheat on principle and whose aunt is a friend of the Franklins' through the Church, the Republicans and the Women's Club. That's how they'd met. The Harvard nephew visits his aunt, the aunt takes him on her Club rounds one day, Francesca accompanies her mother to deliver some cookies to the same charity, and like a drunk swerving over the centre-stripe, there'd been a horrible, utterly unnecessary collision, resulting in marriage.

The relatives have gathered. The neighbourhood girls, the brides-maids, have been in and out all day, brushing past the two college boys in fancy clothes playing chess but not really moving pieces.

Alex remembers his last time with her, the only chance conferred by the gods to thwart her fate. Three weeks before, she'd spoken to him on a Saturday morning, after breakfast. He'd slept over that night and been poking around the silent kitchen for cereal. He'd not known about a wedding, no one had mentioned it. Buzz wasn't a fiancé yet. There still was time to disallow this infatuation with a tall good-looking guy who'd decided to spend his summer in Pittsburgh working at the Mellon Bank instead of New York in securities. Still time to stand in the middle of the track and raise his hand against the 20th Century Limited, stopping it inches from her trussed-up body.

'Alex? Would you do me a big favour?'

She was dressed in a Harvard sweatshirt many sizes too large, in blue jeans, with her hair tied back in a pony-tail. 'I've got a doctor's appoint-ment downtown.' She held out the keys to their family car. She'd never learned to drive. All the other Franklins could have been issued licences in the first grade.

He knew their family doctor, but this one was different. She didn't seem concerned, but what kind of illness requires a Saturday appoint-ment on Diamond Street? He could never stare directly at her as he wanted to, but he had the impression of unusual pallor, a bit of fatigue about the eyes. She'd come in past midnight the night before. Up on the third floor, Alex had heard it. Terry had timed it, from the arrival of the car to the opening of the door. Fifty-seven minutes, a record, he said. 'How time flies when you're having fun.'

He parked on the street, not difficult on a Saturday morning, and waited for her in the car. It was like a date. It was almost like a marriage. She trusted him with something, his discretion, though he sensed it was more. He feared she was in pain, even as he sat there, helpless and ignorant. Or that she was at this moment undressing before a man who would slide a stethoscope between her breasts. He thought of the word 'disrobe' and shivered.

She was back in twenty minutes, surprised, it seemed, that he'd even waited. 'I could have taken the streetcar back.' She seemed almost angry.

'I wanted to.'

'Why?'

The words *I love you* almost came out. They were as close to his lips as they'd ever been. 'What else am I going to be doing? I may as well haul you around.'

'How very gallant we are this morning. All I had to do was get my thing fixed.'

'What thing?'

'So I could use it later,' she laughed. 'That's between us. Now home, please, Alex.'

When they were on the Duquesne Bridge she said, out of the silence that he'd been wanting to break, 'I've always wondered about something – will you give me an honest answer?' It was a warm day, but his hands turned icy.

'About what?'

'You. Promise you won't get angry.'

'You couldn't get me angry.'

'Okay, then. What I've always wanted to know is, how can you *stand* to come over to our house, week after week? Are you a masochist or something? I really want to know.'

He'd been preparing himself to confess his love, his parents' crimes, his collusion. But this, the foundation of his very existence? 'I like your place.'

'*Really?*'

'I want a family just like yours. I *want* to be like your father –'

'Really?'

'A wife, I mean, a marriage, like –'

'You want a wife like my mother? Honestly?'

'Well –'

'Tell me.'

They were just entering the Fort Pitt Tunnels. It is one of the scenes he will carry for life, every stone-face etched, the heaped red lights of a dozen cars dribbling before him into the dark. He can hear his voice even now, an adolescent delivering Cyrano, all the worse because they are true, precisely his feelings.

'I want a wife, just like you.'

Let me die, he thought. Let an avalanche come down. '*You're* why I come. It's only to see you. It's always just to see you.' And then they were in the tunnel, one of those perfectly innocent natural symbols that Pittsburgh especially provides. He needed full control, both hands on the wheel of an unfamiliar station wagon, but he knew it was a moment for reaching out. If they could only stop, he would be met half-way.

Say something, he prayed. They were out of the tunnel. The great truth had been uttered, the burden lifted, and nothing had changed. The same dull yearning, the same wish that he could cut out his tongue.

'I always wondered why you never called me Franny. You always call me Francesca.'

'That's how you were introduced to me. I didn't want to change anything.'

'But I was just a *kid!*'

'Never to me.'

'All those years, and you never even talked to me – I can't believe it. This isn't a joke, is it? What am I, scary?'

'To me you are.'

'What can I say – I'm flattered? I'm sorry? I just never even suspected. You're a good actor, Alex, you really are. Terry always said you didn't like me, and I believed him. He used to tell me the really disgusting names you called me.'

'I couldn't even mention your name.'

'He'd do the same thing to any boy who called me up. No one ever called me a second time. He said everyone figured you'd get around to asking me out, and that would be it. He said he'd work on you to, you know, close your eyes and take me out –'

'Stop it, please. I never, never –'

'That's okay.'

'No, I mean it, I –'

'I said it's all right. I'm not blaming you.' Her voice had changed. 'Terry wants to keep boys away from me and he wants someone he can –'

She broke off, and somewhere inside, his soul did a deep-dive.

'– someone to appreciate him, let's say, so he just found the perfect way of doing it. The worst thing that could possibly have happened was that he'd lose me to you. But you took care of that.'

'I was afraid to speak.'

'He chose you very well. Why not? – he's a very very clever boy. Why do you think *I'm* so friendly with that awful Susan? I want him to find somebody. *Anybody.* We've been together longer than we've been alive, and he won't let go. I suppose he told you about my illness?'

'He said you had some glandular thing.'

'And you believed him I suppose.'

'I didn't want to know.'

'Boy, Alex, if they handed out medals for curiosity. Why *didn't* you ask, if you cared so much? It's the first thing Rodney wanted to know.'

'I was afraid you might have suffered. I couldn't have taken that.'

'I *did* suffer, Alex. I suffered horribly. I had a breakdown. I was a mental case.'

She must have been exaggerating. 'I can't believe that.'

'I wouldn't expect you to. But for one whole year I didn't talk – did Terry tell you that? The doctors said I'd made up my mind that *I* was going to separate us, and the only way I could do it was to kill myself. But I was too young to do it, so I just stopped talking and then I stopped eating just so I wouldn't have to sit beside him in every class for twelve years. Franklin, F. and Franklin, T. like man and wife – I had dreams about school chairs with our names painted on them in blood and that's how the doctors discovered the problem. Does that make sense?'

'Now, yes.'

'Listen to me, Alex, I may be the one who *went* crazy, but he's the crazy one. He's incomplete. He needs another half. If he can't have me, he'll take you. Cut loose, really. I've already got someone, thank God, or else I'd help.'

She was staring out the window, mouth clenched tight, a look he'd seen before, her particular kind of anger. He knew all her looks, he knew so much about her, he thought. He could imagine a smaller version of her, looking out a window for a year in just that clenched silence.

She comes down the stairs early in the afternoon. In white, but the shoulders and bodice are sheathed in such fine muslin she looks, at first, half nude. Terry whistles, Alex whirls in his seat, then turns back to the board. But Terry is advancing on her. 'Best man gets a kiss, right?' and she backs up a step. 'Terry, for heaven's sake, I have to make a phone call.'

'You can call, who's stopping you?' and Alex hears again, against the pounding of his own heart, 'My *make-up*, Terry, God! What's the matter with you today?' and when Alex finally stands and takes a step towards them, he sees his friend, hands on her shoulders, but slowly, playfully, tracing the patterns of white flowers while she stands, nearly his height, a step above him.

'Not bad. Nice work. Don't make 'em like this any more.'

'Ter-ry.'

'No, sir. They broke the sister mould when they made you. But don't tell me all *this* is real.' His hand is lower now, at the point where the solid satin joins the fine mesh, the point of greatest prominence, and his fingers make ever-smaller circles, looking for the sweetest place to land.

Alex takes his cue from the look of panic on her face. She pushes her brother, and Alex grabs his shoulder, and the effect is of a blind-side tackle. Terry has braced himself against her, but from Alex's touch he crumples, down one step and then down two more, falling heavily against the closet door like the villain in a Western fight, as though an enormously strong hero has picked him up and tossed him like a straw against the wall.

Terry says nothing; he's too well-bred. He smiles. A little horseplay, he might be saying, a payback for those hundreds of lost games of chess, Monopoly, Horse and anything else they've ever competed in. Leverage and surprise, and Terry has been humiliated for the first time in his life. Alex feels sure he'll hear about it in some other way.

'You must have been lifting weights, old friend,' he says, rubbing his neck. 'You pack a nasty wallop.' He's taken a small cut on his forehead. The plaster is dented in several places.

'Oh, come on, Terry. It's *her* day. She deserves respect.'

'She deserves,' says Terry, looking at his watch, then at his sister talking urgently on the phone, 'she deserves whatever she's going to get in approximately three hours and twenty-two minutes, depending on traffic. And don't you wish it was you.'

'Come on.'

'Don't you wish you *could*. Don't you wish –' Then he drops it, with a smile. 'Well, wishing won't make it so. Or grow.'

'Terry, watch it.'

'Watch it? What's it going to do?'

'I'll fight you.'

Terry squares his shoulders but doesn't bother to put up his fists. 'Okay, I'm the host and you're the guest. Anything you want, any time you want it. That's the rule around here. At least, it always has been.'

Francesca whirls around, cheeks fiery, as though she'd been slapped.

'Terry! Alex! This is my wedding day – what do you think you're doing?' She shakes her brother. 'Get a hold of yourself. How long are you going to be like this?'

'How long?' he asks in a voice of sweet reasonableness. 'Gee, I wouldn't know. You ought to know by now.'

'You're disgusting. Talk to him, Alex. He's in one of his spells.' Very deliberately, she slaps him, a noise sharper than his crash into the closet door. 'Isn't best man good enough for you? Do you want me to ask Alex? Is that it?'

'I don't want to be your best man,' he says.

'Best man would in his case require a very complicated explanation,' says Terry.

'You shut up. I won't have you ruining the happiest day of my life.'

'And having him up front wouldn't?'

'Of course it wouldn't. I'd prefer it. I should have asked him from the beginning. Alex, will you please be our best man? Rod won't mind.'

'No,' he repeats.

'Honestly, he'd love it. Please, Alex, I can explain it.'

'Yep, good old Buzz thinks you're real Harvard material. "There's one that got away", that's what good old Buzz always says.'

'No,' he says again. He's staring into her face, just inches away.

'I've got an idea!' Terry interjects. 'Let *me* explain it to good old Buzz. Let me explain to him why I shouldn't be best man but my old buddy Alex should be. Would you trust me? Huh, sis?'

'*Sis*,' she repeats, a hiss. 'God, I hate you.'

'Only sometimes.'

Just then, a gaggle of her high-school friends, all dressed in pink and beige formal dresses appear at the head of the stairs. 'Frannie, get up here! He's come! You can't let him see you!'

Her colour drains, she smiles, kisses her fingers and lays them on Alex's lips, then, reluctantly, on Terry's. 'May the better man win,' she whispers, then hikes her train for a quick ascent.

He's out in the backyard an hour later, by the flower bed under the crabapple tree – the fruits are starting to redden – where some of the uncles and cousins have tapped in the croquet wickets and are having a game. They are due at the church in about two hours, but there is time for family and guests, the people without formal duties. He is in his black satiny coat and grey vest, holding a dainty cup of Hawaiian punch. Terry has left for the church with his parents and Rod's family. Griff, one of Terry's younger uncles, is standing at the far corner of the yard, cupping a cigarette. He's the odd man in the family, reportedly a union man from West Virginia, married to Mrs Franklin's much younger sister. He's in his late twenties, wearing a Madras sports coat. Of all people, Buzz is standing with him, tapping his shoes with the end of a croquet mallet.

'Gotta get goin' soon,' Griff is saying. 'Whatya say, Alex?'

'Hey, Alex – great seeing you!' Buzz sweeps a paw in the general direction, and comes up with most of Alex's palm and wrist.

'Congratulations in advance.'

'Griff's giving me some pointers, here. Old married man, and all. Not every day a man gets married, you know.'

'You just missed a garden snake,' says Griff. 'Probably scared him when we started knocking croquet balls into the creepers.'

'Do you think Frannie's afraid of snakes, Alex?' Buzz asks. He stoops from the knees, not looking in his direction. 'You having known her so much longer, I mean.'

'You should ask her,' Alex says, and just then Buzz's hand darts out into the creepers and he snaps to attention with a two-foot garter snake clasped firmly behind the head. What kind of man catches a snake? He holds it out, like a man measuring a belt, and runs his other hand down its length, pinching it at the tail and flipping it over, letting the head hang down nearly to the grass. Actually, Francesca is terrified of snakes. Alex wonders if Buzz intends to shock her with one, a notion he endorses. He has a small, vanishing interest in the quick dissolution of their marriage.

Rod observes in a low voice to Griff and Alex, as he casually twirls the snake in slow arcs, attracting the stares and applause of some of the family, that he's always envied snakes. 'Just think, Griff, if you're a snake, every move you make in the grass could be an orgasm – ever think of that?'

He whirled the snake overhead, higher and faster, like a lariat, then let it go, an airborne eel against the summer sky. They chuckle their appreciation.

'Reckon we know what's on your mind,' says Uncle Griff.

'Boy!' he says, smiling modestly. 'If I don't see you again, Alex, it's been great. Frannie thinks the world of you.'

'And I of her,' he says.

Sitting Shivah
with Cousin Benny

1. ... he could sell anything

My mother's much younger sister, Grace – almost her daughter, almost my older sister – married three times. Her first marriage, to Talbot Ahearn, happened before I can remember and ended when I was ten. Grace was seventeen and a virgin and Uncle Talbot was from the parish and not too Polish; it should have worked. When to enter the holy state of matrimony was a matter of intricate timing, my mother said, like watching the jump rope in a game of hot pepper and timing your leap into it. If it didn't happen in the summer of high school, *it* might never happen, meaning one of those high-school-sweetheart marriages, with the traditional bachelor party and your best friends from childhood as bridesmaids and ushers and best man, and producing a baby by your first anniversary. It would have worked except for Korea, which gave Uncle Talbie an excuse to walk out on a nineteen-year-old wife and two baby girls and to finish his adolescence ten thousand miles from home. It might still have worked but for the fact that Aunt Grace ripened in the two years Uncle Talbie was in Korea and Japan. When he came back he started beating her on account of rumours.

Number Two was a West Virginian named 'Hill' Billy Macdonald, a friend of Uncle Talbie's from the barracks in Korea. Uncle Hill had that snakehipped, sunken look of a career drinker, although he didn't get started till later. He said he got turned on by Aunt Grace from hearing her letters being read out loud by Uncle Talbie. In particular, he remembered two big zeroes along the sides of every page, like unpunched holes of a two-ring binder. It drove him mad wondering what they stood for, until one night in a wet dream, the answer came. 'You dog,' he said, waking Uncle Talbie up. 'I done figured it out. They what I think they are?'

'God, you're slow, Hill,' said Uncle Talbie. Now he knew why Uncle Talbie liked to hold those letters sideways and kissed them before he read.

'Mind if I hold that letter?' He held it up, then against his chest. 'It's her titties, ain't it? You reckon she lets her titties brush against the paper and then takes a pencil out and draws them little circles around – oh, God, man, like to drive me crazy!'

'Gotta leave something for the imagination, Hill.'

'Jesus God, where'd you find a woman like that?'

These were still young men, soldiers in a country they hated. What's a boy to do, what runs through his mind, brushing his lips where the nipples of an unglimpsed lady love had just been pressed? It was unnatural for all of them, including Aunt Grace, having to live with her disapproving older sister and brother-in-law. None of this would have happened if Uncle Talbie had stayed with the roads department, and if Uncle Hill hadn't been roped in by all those letters and if Aunt Grace hadn't had to go out and find the only kind of job a good-looking twenty-year-old with two little kids in 1952 could find, which inevitably led to meeting older men after hours.

So many odd things wait in our futures, lined up like rides in an amusement park, parked and freshly painted and inviting us to climb aboard. You think you're headed for a restful interlude in the tunnel of love, but it's a roller coaster, you know the minute you feel that cranking under your seat and you open your eyes and all you can see are clouds. You're in the front seat without a safety belt.

And none of it would have happened if Aunt Grace hadn't been a gifted letter-writer with a special talent for naive spontaneity. Maybe she learned from the movies of the day and cultivated the voice and manner of those wiser-than-they-look post-war blondes with cynical insouciance. She was usually blond and a little hard-edged. If she hadn't advertised disappointment and availability between the lines as well as along the sides of her letters, and if Uncle Hill, whom no one ever credited with much sensitivity, hadn't possessed a brief moment of empathy he would later call love, there would be no Benny. Later on, Hill would say what he felt in his heart about Gracie moved him like a country song, and he'd take his guitar and pick at it for hours, trying to find words that never came. All he could sing was 'Amazin' Gracie, you're drivin' me crazy,' but it seemed too blasphemous. He hated his best friend Talbie and would have liked to plug him on the firing range, and he dreamed of knocking on Gracie's door and saying, I'm sorry, ma'am, but I was a friend of your late husband, Talbot Ahearn. I'm here to tell you he made me promise to look after you and your little girls, so if you don't mind, I'll just move in and make you my wife.

When he learned they'd split up, Hill was on the next bus to Aunt Grace's last known address. She was now a divorcée, and with it came a kind of early-fifties allure, the promise of desperation and lowered standards. She was waitressing and hostessing, the sorts of job a chivalrous mountain boy dreams of rescuing a princess from. She was the first divorcée in our family, maybe the first anyone in our family had ever known, and Uncle Hill was desperate to save her reputation.

He came from loose-living hillfolks in the southern part of West Virginia, but everyone said Uncle Hill, early on, before the drinking and the failure of his enterprises, was an upstanding representative. To my mother, it meant Uncle Hill was now good enough for Aunt Grace. She was damaged goods, and he was Protestant. So she and the daughters went down to Huntington for a couple of years while Uncle Hill experimented with chinchillas and then mink and even some silver foxes before she got tired of cleaning up after cuddly rats and smelly weasels. She couldn't take his favourite dessert any more, canned fruit salad poured over a slice of sugared Wonder bread. She hated the way he stubbed out his cigarettes into the mashed potatoes. It made her feel like a waitress again. By then she was twenty-six and the Ahearn girls were growing fast and thank God Uncle Hill had caught some disease in Korea that left him sterile. Aunt Grace came back home to a different part of town, figuring to find something indoor and sanitary, maybe keeping the books in a hardware store. Life had given her a keen understanding of maintenance, and she could repair just about anything and keep major machinery running long past its time.

I was ten years old and starting to catch on to things. She'd gone through two husbands in five years and we didn't have a word, let alone the concept for a double divorcée. She was attractive and outgoing, and the number of new marriages and divorces could only grow over the years. Aunt Grace was leading a Hollywood life.

In our city, call it Pittsburgh, if I said we were South Side and Aunt

Grace became East Side, at least the way it was forty-five years ago, I could just as easily be describing different countries, or at least different states. We had lawns and new houses. Oakland had tall, broad trees and everything the nineteenth century had left behind, including Carnegie Library and Museum, Forbes Field and the universities. Their houses and buildings were brick and stone and stained from the pre-smoke-ordinance years. Ours were wood, and painted pastel. Their trees vaulted over the streets; ours were spindly. They took streetcars. We had new cars, traded every two years. The bridges and tunnels and freeways of Pittsburgh, the aluminum buildings down at the Point were all for us and all about being new and progressive, about outgrowing Pittsburgh's Hunkie and Polack origins. There was something in Aunt Grace that attracted her to Oakland, where she found that indoor job answering phones at a real estate company.

The real Pittsburgh, as I imagined it, housed itself in the East End. Pittsburgh had been the dirtiest city in America, with the ugliest history. But it was also where the Gilded Age had made its money and left its monuments. I went out to Carnegie Museum every weekend, sketched the animals and skeletons, then walked across the parking lot to Forbes Field to take advantage of free admission to Pirates' games after the seventh inning. Oakland was the part of Pittsburgh that Willa Cather wrote about, the only part that Kenneth Burke and Malcolm Cowley could have come from. I longed for their kind of friendship, that it might be possible to exchange books and discuss the fate of the world without having to go to New York. It seemed unfair that Oakland also had the dinosaurs, the paintings, the books, the concert halls, the universities and the stadiums. They even had art movies, where rumours of occasional nudity in Swedish films trickled over to us on the South Side, but usually a day too late, after the authorities had closed them down.

I was an aberration in my family, someone with 'leanings', my parents suspected, which meant anything subversive, any kind of confused or overdeveloped political, sexual, intellectual, artistic or religious urge that might lead to a questioning of the faith, tests of loyalty or outbursts of zealotry. Athletics ruled our high school. Family gossip alone was considered dinner conversation, and business schemes consumed my parents' waking hours. I was a confused and angry twelve-year-old, and even angrier at thirteen. I was a reader, a stamp collector, a moviegoer, a planetarium visitor – anything that spoke of vast distance and remote time. Realities other than the South Side of Pittsburgh earned my traitor's allegiance.

Then, sometime late in the first Eisenhower administration, Aunt Grace met an older salesman named Danny Israel whom she identified as a 'funny guy and a sharp dresser'. My mother said, 'Israel?' and laughed in a way that said, *Silly me, I thought you said Israel.* 'Squirrel Hill?' she asked, as a way of confirming it without actually asking, and Aunt Grace said, Naw, he grew up in Johnstown. 'Danny Israel from Little Israel?' my father persisted, which to him was the whole East End, any place that wasn't black and stayed open on Sunday. 'I guess,' said Aunt Grace, which allowed my parents, reconciled now to the possibility of the whole Judaeo-Christian tradition having suddenly opened up, one new observation apiece. 'At least he won't be a drinker,' my mother said. 'I hear they keep their fists to themselves,' said my father. 'Thanks for your blessing,' said Aunt Grace.

Aunt Grace always said that Uncle Danny could sell anything. He'd survived the Depression by selling; he'd spent four years in the Pacific Theatre selling more than fighting. He was a walking history of twentieth-century commerce, starting with newspapers, encyclopedias and sheet music, and moving on to pharmaceuticals, hardware, gents' suits, musical instruments, cars and appliances. He had finally settled on furniture. He was great with numbers, calculating costs and profits in his head. He could read a department store the way Indian scouts could read the forest. 'Move this here and bring the lighter objects up front,' he'd suggest, and the salesman would jerk a thumb in the direction a supervisor and say, 'Do I look like a shlepper? Tell him.'

From all those jobs he'd picked up lingo and expertise, the way journalists become instant, serial experts. From the advice he gave, people thought he'd gone to medical school; he could tune a piano, he could play any Gershwin halfway decently, and Aunt Grace swore he'd read everything in those encyclopedias he'd sold. From the way she and my mother whispered and giggled out of anyone's earshot, I guessed that Uncle Danny was more than just a sharp dresser, compared to my father or to her earlier husbands. It was the Depression, Aunt Grace said, the need to support old parents, that had deflected him from his chosen course of law. 'No shlepping, that's all I ask,' he'd say, hands up like he was stopping a train, 'First thing I do, any new job, I say "only selling, no shlepping".'

'That means lifting, Dolly,' Aunt Grace would say, our own in-house *shiksa*.

No Shlepp became our nickname for Uncle Danny. 'Hey, Danny-boy,' my father would greet him at the door, 'still not shlepping, are you?' It gave us a grip on an alien world, just being able to say it.

My later memories of Uncle Danny are of post-dinner Sunday afternoons with different radios on in different rooms, music competing with a baseball game or pro football depending on the season, in front of our big black-and-white television set, with my father nodding off and Uncle Danny nursing a beer waiting for the snoring to start so he could turn the channel. In the years before the incomparable Roberto Clemente came to town, Pittsburgh teams were as boring as brown socks. Pitt could go years without winning, the Pirates were the oldest and slowest team in baseball, and the Steelers were as inept a franchise as was ever fielded. We learned to deal with disappointment on a daily basis.

'You know our trouble, Stevie?' he asked me the first time he ever visited as we listened to a Pirates loss on radio. I was getting ready to defend Ralph Kiner. He ticked off the names on the Pirates' roster. 'Abrams, Goodman, Kravitz, Levy – our own local schlimazels, Stevie. Too many of our boys on the field, not enough in the front office.'

Like any good Pittsburgher, I wasn't accustomed to disloyalty. I wanted to defend our boys, the O'Brien twins, the Freese brothers, in the face of all their ineptitude. *They* were 'our boys'. Who were our boys, if not that sorry collection? Who did we think we were – the Yankees? He seemed sceptical of just about everything I revered. Sometimes we'd watch 'The Voice of Firestone', high culture for us South Siders, and I could feel his disdain. In Oakland they had William Steinberg and the Pittsburgh Symphony. Uncle Danny could hum the arias and he even knew the words. 'Worked with a lot of Italians in my day,' he explained. Roberta Peters was the sexiest thing on television. 'Firestone' had the lowest-cut gowns out there. Risë Stevens was as close as the South Side got to Swedish beauty on demand. Cesare Siepi was Aunt Grace's idea of a good-looking guy, but then, so was Uncle Danny despite his Jimmy Durante nose. Sex at the close of the first Eisenhower term was everywhere, if you knew where to look.

Aunt Grace gave birth to my cousin Benny one year after marrying Uncle Danny. 'Short for Benjamin?' my mother asked, determined to make the best of it. Naw, Dolly, said Aunt Grace, Danny just loves Jack Benny. I was fourteen. My mother was forty, Gracie was twenty-six, but already her hair was the colour of stubbled corn fields, flecked with early frost.

2. ... any story we can tell
is a brief parable of the twentieth century ...

Our township had one movie house, set prominently on the main street next to the trolley loop and the bakery. In the mid-fifties people were staying home to watch television. I could have as well, but I went to the movies every night. My parents had started a little business, a lamp store in a strip mall, meaning every school night for me was free and the money they left for supper could just as easily go for popcorn and movies. I never checked the marquee or the starting times. I went in, watched the popcorn swirl from the smoking kettle. No urgency. I bought, I waited for my eyes to adjust, and I sat.

You entered when you liked, movies were continuous, you caught the story on the fly. The story ended where *you'd* come in, narratives held an infinity of beginnings and ends. The pleasure was watching your ending slowly gather itself, scattered elements slowly compose themselves into *your* opening, and then extract added pleasure by staying beyond *your* ending, which was also your beginning, layering the plot in a different way, until it got predictable and boring.

I never knew where the story was heading. I could make up a dozen plots. To take delight in narrative helplessness, would anyone today tolerate it, having to hear every word acutely, having to pay the strictest attention to every detail – and *still* not making a shred of sense out of any of it for the first half hour? A pleasurable surrender to ordered confusion, not knowing a single character, not grasping a story line, sensing only good and evil, marking the expendables and guessing at survivors. I strolled in at four o'clock for the double feature and came out at eight-thirty with plenty of time left for homework.

Film noir was passing, and so was the favourite comedy team of my childhood, Abbott and Costello, to be replaced by the loathsome Martin and Lewis. Westerns were getting broody. Musicals were too bright and dancy. War movies had lost their edge. Black-and-white was passing, except for science fiction. Colour meant fantasy. Men wore narrow ties and bluish-grey suits, they flirted with their secretaries, they schemed and drank and smoked in after-work Manhattan bars. Phil Silvers replaced Oscar Levant. They all dressed like Cary Grant. Women wore wide skirts with thick belts and white blouses with their collars turned up. They wore their hair short and blond. They looked a little like Aunt Grace, and maybe their lives had a lot in common.

I took the same seat every night, back row on the middle aisle. Friends knew where to find me, and I had that nighttime circle of the South Side's kibitzing adolescents who were too good or too smart for street gangs, but not the type for libraries or chemistry sets. We were more the hobbyists. We collected things, and that's what movies were to me, thousands of collector's moments. I learned the world from movies, not television, and maybe I'm the last generation to say that.

And then one day in my senior year of high school, my mother received a stiff cardboard invitation card from Aunt Grace and Uncle Danny. Would we be kind enough to attend the début recital of Benny Israel, soloist with the Pittsburgh Junior Symphony, guest-conducted by William Steinberg himself. He was four years, ten months old.

3. … he was a black hole
sitting on the pianist's bench

Every Sunday for as long as I've been conscious, there's been a 'Prince Valiant' on the comic page. It can't die, it's eternal, and I've never read a single panel. It's beautifully drawn, and the most literate script in the paper, postmodern before there was Postmodernism, new age before there was New Age, camp before there was Camp. With all that mad hair, that costuming, that intricately irrelevant story line, you'd think he'd have his lone, crackpot, visionary advocates, but no one talks about him, he has no explicators. Even Krazy Kat has its exegetes. What mad consortium thought him up, who pitches his story every week, who keeps churning him out? Who pays for it? Has *anyone* ever read 'Prince Valiant?' It's too late for me to start, too much has gone on, I can't enter

that theatre any more. In some way I feel I'm not good enough for
Prince Valiant, just like I wasn't good enough for 'The Voice of Firestone' or the East Side of Pittsburgh or for Cousin Benny.

We hadn't known about the seriousness of Benny's music. Aunt
Grace never boasted about him, only that he sure loved banging on his
piano and she was thinking of going back to work to help pay for extra
lessons. The Israels were always busy on Sundays, they wouldn't come
over, wouldn't go for drives with us. Snickers turned to dark mutterings
of their having changed, of avoidance, of conversion. In the summer,
they wouldn't rent a cabin next to us in Cooke Forest. 'The boy' hated
the woods, and then he was subject to hayfever and mosquito bites, he
needed special foods, and he couldn't live a week separated from his
piano teacher.

'What next?' my mother would ask. 'Where does a healthy boy get
those ideas?' Allergies, to her, were just another 'leaning' to be swatted
down. Obviously, there was something wrong with Cousin Benny. We'd
always asked about his lessons, but that was mere politeness. When he
did come over on Sundays, he'd prowl our house for a piano and then
for records, but all he found were Fred Waring and Bing Crosby albums.

What could be expected of crazy Gracie and her Moshe Dayan?
William Steinberg himself conducting – wasn't that a bit la-di-da? He
should be out in the fresh air riding a bike. He couldn't catch or throw,
he didn't play games, he couldn't stand television. He sneered at 'The
Voice of Firestone.' Why let voices ruin perfectly good music? he said.
He carried his school books and sheet music pressed against his chest,
like a girl. He was scary. A normal Benny sentence would start, 'If what
you say is true...,' as if he'd caught us disputing a law of nature, and the
sentence would wrap itself around a 'then', and march to a confident,
syllogistic end. If what you say is true, then all things are possible. Or
futile.

It's natural for an only child to look at his cousin, his genetic quarter,
and try to see a brother, some sort of genetic confluence, a potential yet
to achieve, a temptation to put aside. In my case, there'd be no one closer
to me in the universe, apart from my parents, whom I'd long dis-
counted, and Aunt Grace. And yet, what did I see that night of his debut
at Shriner's Temple – I, a seventeen-year-old high school senior with
good grades and a tolerant attitude – but a black hole of a boy, a smudge

on the bench in front of a huge piano, from which no light, no joy, just notes, burst forth? We were not of the same universe, my cousin and I, maybe not parallel galaxies, and the thought made me miserably unhappy. I was the one who went to the planetarium, the one who wished to be wrapped in infinity. And here it was, my cousin, infinitely ahead of me. I wanted to claim him.

The first time cousin Benny showed his special brain, he was sitting between us on the sofa, staring at a football game. He might have been three, and he'd never watched a down of football in his life. He took in a couple of offensive series and then piped up, 'Third and two!'

'That's a smart little boy you've got there, Danny-boy,' said my father. 'How'd he know that?' My mother was convinced most Steeler fans had to use their fingers.

'Oh, he's quick with numbers, this one,' said Uncle Danny. But I remembered Uncle Danny's own ability and the logic teasers he'd bring over on Sundays. It wasn't just 43 percent of any price, he could do magic tricks with numbers. For him, the world was one big spinning disc of numbers.

I had another indication that Cousin Benny was smart, smart, again from football. Benny was seven and I was home from college. I liked him, he was weird and wondrous, and you could see the world pouring in through his eyes and ears. You could watch some higher force processing it. 'Explain this scoring to me,' he commanded. We were watching the day's football scores scrolling down the television screen. He'd noted the repetitions, the multiples of seven. 'What's nice about football,' I explained, 'is that every score except 1-0 is possible.' I described safeties and field goals, touchdowns and extra points. 'Theoretically,' I said, employing another Bennyism, 'an infinity of scores is possible, except for 1-0.'

'Actually, if what you say is true ...' *It is, it is, you troll.* I wanted to strangle him. '... then your infinity-minus-one case is false. The possible number of scores is closer to zero than infinity. From your own logic it follows that there cannot be 2-1, a 3-1, a 4-1... 35-1 score, or anything like it.'

I was twenty, I was in college, dating, driving a goddamn car.

I don't want it thought that I wasn't a good student, or that I was totally unaware of the dynamics of my age. I was a great student. But I was a South Hills High School student and the opportunities for college weren't too broad. I could think of Pitt or Duquesne, or maybe even Carnegie Tech, with Penn State in reserve. It was clear that I would be the first in my family to go to college, simply because I was of the first generation for whom the refusal to join the father's world, his trade, his union, was not considered an act of betrayal.

In my junior year of high school, I'd helped to organize a chess squad. We couldn't use the word 'team', since that was reserved for contact sports. Chess had become an obsession in the summer days between my sophomore and junior years. My imaginary opponent was Cousin Benny, who, so far as I knew, did not play chess and never would, if I had anything to say about it. It's possible to go from a rank beginner to near-ranked chess player in a year of decent competition, and by my junior year, I had organized my nightly movie group into a chess squad. 'Squad' is better than 'team'. It suggests commando raids. The first school I thought of calling for competition was Taylor-Allderdice, in Squirrel Hill. In my senior year, I'd finally found a legitimate excuse for taking those cranking old Pittsburgh streetcars over to Squirrel Hill, to walk their streets, to meet their best students, the interested teachers, and to drop in on my family, the Israels, for dinner two or three nights a week.

4. ... and now for something completely different ...

Kenneth Burke, the literary critic, was a hero to me, living as he did, writing as he did about topics no one had thought about, and coming from Pittsburgh's Gilded Age. Most of the times I'd seen him, at professional meetings, he was dead drunk. When he died at ninety-six, deep in the age of postmodernity, the cause according to the *Times* obituary was 'heart failure'. It was a simple-minded definition of failure. He'd died, if anything, of heart success. It raised questions of what constitutes success and failure: must failure always be associated with death?

I did well enough in college to become, in my own way, an intellectual. I make my living by reading books, by teaching books, by writing on books. I've known marriage and fatherhood, earned some recognition, piled up some guilt, and reach occasionally, but never too strenuously, for redemption. But this is not about me. If anything, it's about living through fifty years of life in this country, being the kid who entered the movie at any time and sat there, waiting for resolution.

This story is about *perestroika.*

How do you top a concert debut at four years ten months? Perhaps you don't. You become famous simply for being a prodigy, a Yehudi Menuhin. At the time we didn't think of prodigies as anything but successes with a head start. We thought of Benny as our own Roberto Clemente, precociously gifted in every aspect of his game, destined for greatness, for redemption of a city, or in our case, a family. Benny continued to be known in Pittsburgh for at least twenty years. He won every local piano competition, he spent his summers in the music camps, he received a scholarship to Juilliard, he studied with names I might have heard of even if I didn't have a special family interest. And yet, Benny never quite made it, and in his series of second- and third-places finishes in the major European competitions, people read burn-out and failure. If he'd been a phenom of eighteen or twenty there would have been tours, recording contracts, but by eighteen, Benny was a veteran. He'd lost his cuteness and he'd never be a beauty; he'd missed his chance at a title shot.

I was living in North Carolina when our parents began dying. Benny had stayed in Pittsburgh, on a music faculty, giving some lessons, playing in the Light Opera. I saw him at my father's funeral, then, unexpectedly, at Aunt Grace's, dead of cancer at fifty-five. Uncle Danny didn't live too much longer and the services took me to my first Shivah, my first yarmulke, in their Squirrel Hill home amidst his paternal relatives I'd never met. Uncle Danny's brothers and sisters, up from Florida, the ones who'd not be derailed by the Depression, the lawyers and accountants. So *this* is what made him different from me, I thought, that tiny difference that sent me to the movies, to Forbes Field, and him to the concert stage. 'You look good in it, Stevie,' Benny said, 'it covers that little bald spot.' His cheeks were stubbly, his figure bent. A wide swath of baldness cut across the top of his head. I was forty-four, which made him about thirty. He was an orphan now, and his father had left him a trust fund, recognizing, perhaps, that his lone failure had been not endowing Benny's gifts with any kind of fallback. If he was not to become the towering genius of our age, he might have to end up a taxi driver, except, of course, that he didn't know how to drive.

Five years later, I heard, he'd left teaching – and Pittsburgh. Someone said he'd joined the government, and I remember thinking, if the government still absorbs and swallows geniuses like Benny Israel, it must be working at a higher level than any casual criticism can justify. He was my last link to an American urban experience that I'd come to view as great, in the profundity of its divisions, the sheer will of its public monuments, its guilty endowments, at least in the years that I had known it.

Cut now to recent history. Benny and I are both orphans, and worse, I'm a twice-divorced orphan with kids scattered around the country cursing my name. All I can say in my defence is that I never ceased being that boy in the back row of the theatre who wandered into stories and began milking them for sense, demanding that they send a million little messages of comprehension for those of us who came in deprived of context or preparation. That's not a bad beginning for the practice of any kind of criticism, and over the years it's become the core of my method, such as it is. They call it 'de-privatizing' the narrative, I'm suddenly the founder of the Deprivatizing School. I have become the spokesman for all readers and viewers who ever felt themselves deprived by a work of art.

All of which takes me to places here and abroad. I keep a suitcase packed, my passport up to date. It took me from North Carolina to New York. It took me to the Soviet Union just before it became Russia again, and a host of new republics, to lecture from Tallinn to Kiev for the State Department, with longer stops in then-Leningrad and Moscow. The cultural affairs officer, in inviting me, said that in the chaos of those Soviet times, every day in Moscow was like reading chapters from *The Deprived Reader* and *Leftovers to Live By*, on the impossibility of master texts in a postmodern age. *Every* day was like entering a foreign movie whose language you didn't know, halfway through. The last short paragraph mentioned that a cousin of mine, Benny Israel, had recently joined the cultural office, and sent his regards.

5. ... I stroll the streets of Moscow with Cousin Benny ...

You live long enough and nothing is strange, my cousin was explaining. Gone were the old Bennyisms, the arrogance and confidence, the suppressed hostility of even a simple sentence. He was overjoyed to see me – what if I'd refused, remembering him as an obnoxious squirt? He'd read my books, he followed me on the Internet, he pressed my books on everyone wherever he was posted. How did I do it, he wanted to know. Of all the things in the world he admired, to have come up with a theory!

'There's no theory, Benny. All I've ever written about is what being an adolescent in Pittsburgh felt like. The rest is footnotes.'

'I envy you that,' he said.

In a part of the city that could have been Moscow's Squirrel Hill, he took me to a coffee shop where people recognized him. His Russian seemed fluent, one of those talents we hadn't perfected at home. The black tea was strong; he sipped his from a glass, through a sugar cube. Maybe it wasn't just baldness and near middle age that had mellowed him, or the apparent abandonment of a musical career. It might just have been the Zeitgeist, Moscow in *perestroika*, the surrender of ego in what might be, miracle of miracles, a benign revolution. Maybe Moscow was the Pittsburgh he'd never had. His ego, or at least the one I loved and feared, was gone.

'I have a girlfriend here. If they try to transfer me, I may stay.'

I remembered the trust fund. The state of the ruble made a million-aire of any dollar-holder. 'What's she like?' I asked, trying to banish the thoughts of a Marina Oswald. I'd been in this city before, back in the deadly seventies in the brutal hands of Intourist guides named Lyud-mila, when I'd been watched, turned away from scholars I'd tried to call, given official tickets to every boring cultural event to keep me off the streets, when nothing was permitted. Moscow was the City of Dreadful Nyet. I could imagine Benny falling for the first woman who took him in. He wasn't my cousin any more; he was my son, my little brother.

We walked through a neighbourhood of old trees and yellow apart-ment blocks. He lived nearby, he said, meaning that his Yelena did, since he was still inside the American compound. She was an underpaid doctor with children, two bad marriages, a love of music, some talent in singing and acting. One of her sons hoped to go to Conservatory. We passed an old theatre where beggars sat under the marquee holding signs that mentioned Afghanistan. According to the marquee, the show had the longest title I'd ever seen, not that I could read a word.

'The hottest ticket in Moscow,' said Benny. He looked up, and pointed at each Cyrillic clump as he translated. '"PERESTROIKA IS AN OLD HOTEL IN SVERDLOVSK AND KURT VONNEGUT, JR., IS A BELLHOP INSIDE IT." Roughly,' he said, then continued. 'A revue, starring Lazar Israelovitch and Yelena Vaingurt. There's a subtitle. "SHIVAH FOR MOTHER RUSSIA."' I caught the smile of distant proprietorship. 'You of course have to picture Kurt Vonnegut, Jr., with a silver tooth in the front of his mouth, dressed like Trotsky and speaking with a Sverdlovsk accent.'

'I see Oscar Levant,' I said. 'You must feel reborn, Mr Israelovitch.'

'Pittsburgh boy, Oscar,' he said. 'My father knew him, way back in Fifth Avenue High.'

Yelena's apartment building had once been fancy, remained imposing, but lacked amenities, beginning with new glass in the front door whose lock had been wrenched off its wooden frame. No lobby lights, no elevator, no hall lights. But once inside, her place was a pleasant retreat with an almost wooded view of treetops, a piano that took up all the parlour, a bookshelf of thick texts, tables heaped with medical magazines.

'Journals, research. Life goes on, you see.' Yelena was at work. Benny left her a message in Russian, filled a glass bowl with Hershey's Kisses, and dropped two red apples on her kitchen table.

Then he sat at the piano. 'Yelena sings most of the songs, I write the jokes. What do you think of this?' He started playing 'September Song', then 'Mack the Knife'. I remembered Uncle Danny playing Gershwin. 'Of course I wouldn't go on this long just with the music. It's like Jack Benny and his violin, or Victor Borge at the piano – remember him on Ed Sullivan, those Sundays in Pittsburgh?' Did he remember those Firestone nights, I wondered, was he watching television all the time that I thought he was watching, and judging, us? 'I start with a little "September Song" and Yelena comes bursting in. Make like you're Yelena. Read this.' He handed me a slip of paper. I was about to protest I didn't read Russian, but there were only three words, in English.

'With a "V" remember,' he said.

'Vas Kurt Weill?'

'Not *vas* Kurt Weill? Was Kurt *Veill*?'

I tried it again.

'Weill? Oh, he was despicable!' cried Cousin Benny, with a crescendo of mangled Weill notes, then calmed down. He put on his wire glasses and a little peaked cap. Trotsky with a silver tooth. He launched into a classical riff, something I didn't recognize. 'Did Gustav Mahler?' he asked.

'What?'

'Mahler? Dey vusn't even in the same room!'

I went to the performance that night. Yelena was plump and blond and though she and Benny spoke in Russian, her English was nearly flawless. Yelena indulged Benny his Russian, Benny indulged Yelena her glamour on stage, where she lost her years and heaviness. Her voice was young. Her musical son played saxophone behind the curtain. Cousin Benny may have looked like a passable provincial Trotsky, but when he spoke familiar words of Lenin and Stalin, Brezhnev and Gorbachev in an exaggerated Odessa accent, and the occasional, 'and so it goes', I still missed the cigarette and the sturdy sourness of Oscar Levant. The audience roared its recognition, laughed in the right places, and I realized the world was fast becoming a thoroughly crazy place.

6. … we find our beginning, in our end

Cousin Benny is a failure. What else can we call a genius born without theory, born without the competitive fire? To mount a cabaret in Moscow – compared with debuting at five with the Pittsburgh Junior Symphony under the direction of William Steinberg himself?

He stayed on in Moscow for another three years but he didn't marry Yelena. He finally accepted a new rotation, this time to Sri Lanka, where again he arranged for me to visit. His perfect Russian is rusting a bit, though he still has Russian friends and enjoys movies at the Russian cultural centre. His Sinhalese is perking right along. He runs the show in Colombo, a troubled post under bomb threat where he receives hardship pay. He's rented a beachfront bungalow under a row of palms. There is a local woman, a half-Polish, half-Sinhalese journalist, known for her conciliatory attitude toward Tamils. He is trying to arrange a conference next year, bringing American minority artists to Colombo and Jaffna, to define the limits of ethnic consciousness. He has a new cause: educating majorities who behave defensively, like minorities; all the peoples of the world who treat their minorities as hostile majorities just over a border. Sinhalese, Serbs, Israelis, Quebeckers.

He sits in a long canvas slingchair under available light, reading local papers, consuming stacks of local novels, and in the evenings sometimes gives Gershwin concerts for his friends. He's taken up a new hobby, photography, and turns the lens on himself each morning. The walls are filled with self-portraits, seven hundred so far, hoping to capture the secret of the aging process. Already he has remarked the differences, in grey hairs, in wrinkles, in neck sag, in little vertical creases, between his day of arrival and just two years later. He intends to keep it going for the rest of his life.

The Waffle Maker

1. Where the Myths Touch Us

Around the turn of the last century my grandfather, Morris Loewe, opened a pawnshop a few doors from a burlesque house on Diamond Street at the corner of Smithfield. The brass section, 'long on breath, short on funds', often needed quick cash. Dented trumpets and big brass slide trombones helped finance his first twenty years in America. One of his regular clients wrote a catchy little tune about a pawnshop, on a corner, in Pittsburgh, Pennsylvania.

My father, Lou Morris, hung around the burlesque, singing and dancing, picking up piano, the saxophone and trumpet, dropped out of school, and finally caught on, singing backup with Como and Eckstine. In dance school he worked up a little routine with a klutzy kid named Gene Kelly. Years later, acting as a talent scout for his own radio show, he'd been the first to book Dino Crocetti, a pouty teenager from the locally infamous town of Steubenville.

That magical generation, except for Lou Morris, left Pittsburgh when they were still young enough to change their names and scrub away the accent. They'd send my father elaborate Christmas cards and when they came back home on tour or family business, they'd include him on their weekend 'retreats'. He'd return with new glossies of the stars' night out. He was the bald man at the edge of the picture, next to young blond women in dresses with plunging necklines, their cigarettes held high, tall drinks set before them. 'Oh, Lou, really, they're so cheap-looking,' my mother would say. Over the years, our game-room walls came to resemble a Times Square deli, every inch covered with glossies of dimmed or forgotten celebrities and their painfully brash inscriptions. I wondered back then how they kept their names straight, what it's like being famous as someone they never were.

Now, it's my San Francisco friends who pronounce the photos 'archival'. *Isn't that …? Jeez, it looks like a really young Dean Martin!* they ask of the pouty boy in a long white jacket cradling a microphone the size of a twenty-four-hour lollypop. I kept my father's poster-sized Gene Kelly in straw hat and cane, signed: *To my old buddy Lou. Thanks for carrying me, Gino.* In front of that poster, in the game room, my father installed a raised stage under a spotlight, four feet on a side, made from boards saved after the demolition of their old dance school.

'Fred Astaire,' he'd snort. 'What does it say about me?' My father was better looking, a better singer, and even the better tap-dancer. The problem was in the geographical coordinates of his life. To stay where fate had spawned you was to invite the question, 'If you're so good, why are you still here?' Astaire didn't stay Freddie Austerlitz and he and his sister got the hell out of Omaha as fast as they could. *You can be a second-rate talent in a first-class city – that's normal,* an old friend once told him. *But you sure as hell can't be a first-rate talent in a third-rate market.* Pittsburgh was the very definition of third-rate, a dirtier, remoter Philadelphia, a joke-butt town with talent drain and losing teams.

When television came to Pittsburgh, local producers were challenged to find ways of filling vast stretches of raw time. For fifteen years, my father had been hosting a popular talent-scout show on local radio; and the station was desperate to shift it to television. But when compared with the sophistication of Pittsburgh radio – the oldest in the world, after all – the early years of local television were crude and shlocky. Every local market developed its Pinky Lee, Soupy Sales or Lou Morris, big-time talent with city-wide fame. But my father had his dignity. He modelled himself on Ted Mack, not Milton Berle. No seltzer, no wigs, no floppy shoes, no drag. No shtick.

Then one day in rehearsal a young director shouted into the boom, 'Do that again, Lou!' The cameramen and floor directors were convulsed in laughter, pointing to their ears. And that is the way I remember him: a bald man – Adlai Stevenson bald – exploiting a recessive chromosomal gift, an ear-hinge that permitted a wiggle, singly and in tandem, in and out, up and down, even in circles. And with the helicopter ears he learned ventriloquism and created a smartass singing hand puppet named Mister Foystinger. There had been talk of getting him on Sullivan until Ed resurrected one of his undead, a Spaniard with a cigarette-smoking hand puppet. Señor Wences ruined it for any other bald ventriloquist over fifty. He made it once on *Arthur Godfrey and His*

Friends. What a joke, he said. That son of a bitch has no friends.

This business exacts a price. Your dignity if you're lucky, but usually your soul. My father believed that tap-dancing was the pinnacle of American art, noble in all its aspects. Something tragic had happened. An American art form had passed into the hands of Hollywood and Ed Sullivan. Hollywood had never been richer, but where were the new kids? Even the Negro clubs in the Hill District were depleted. So, if tap is your art, and tap is dead, why not make a monkey of yourself, why not throw your voice and wiggle your ears? The body is still the greatest instrument.

I chose the name Lew Morrison. For the past thirty years I've been living in San Francisco, writing scripts. One was about an old tap-dancer so crippled with phlebitis, double hip replacement, and legs so brittle from bone-chips and arthritis that he could barely lift them from the ottoman. Still, one night he rises, goes to his shoe-closet, and under a spell, alone, dances.

2. In Search of Lost Time

I'm sitting in the airport-bound Super Shuttle in the pre-dawn darkness of a San Francisco winter, having surrendered my consciousness to higher authorities, heading east. This van-driver and then the pilot have taken charge of my life. It's heaven. No one can reach me, and I can't call out. My father never saw California. I don't know why these memories are pressing in on me. I'm heading east with a play that will open off-Broadway in three months. I'm at the peak of my powers, yet here I sit, sixty years old in a van and thinking of my father's wiggling ears. As we crawl over the hills of San Francisco picking up busy young passengers, as I listen to fragments of conversations, I think with sudden amazement and some gratitude that on this morning I personally command over half a century of history. Even my youngest brothers and sisters, last seen when they were babies, would be middle-aged.

This play is my late-term declaration of artistic independence. One actor on a bare stage confronting the voices and judgement of history. *The Principle of Uncertainty,* it's called, starring that old crypto-fascist, Werner Heisenberg, the first to tell the world that we can know a particle's position, or its velocity, but not both. Ramifications are endless.

It's the great unwelcome discovery of the twentieth century. We can know where, but not when. *We cannot know.* Heisenberg opted for certainty in his own peculiar way.

At the newspaper kiosk just before the security check I bought my *Times* and *Chronicle,* usually enough to see me through a cross-continental flight. This time, however, I noticed the plastic-sleeved covers of *Playboy* and a smiling face in a Pilgrim's hat and an unbuttoned black cape. And yes, I'm as curious as any college boy about the hidden topography. But I know her. I wrote her first movie. She went to Brown and played a memorable Juliet in the Park. She painted, sang, danced. Her mother was a doctor, her father a professor, and her agent, obviously, a pig. She would be draped nude inside for every college boy and every old man she ever trusted, but if I dared to take it off the rack I know I'd be spotted. Some old friend would step from behind the display case with a high-minded Bay Area book in his hand. He'd say nothing, but he'd look at me forever in a new light. And I can imagine the two Indian girls at the counter giggling to each other. *What is that old fool going to do with that magazine?* I have my dignity. I pay for the papers and hope for a challenging crossword.

In the wide, middle aisle between the moving walkways, airport authorities maintain an ever-changing mini-museum of twentieth-century gadgets and marvels. On my last trip there was a Bakelite Festival, including the same purple clock radio I'd wakened to as a boy. I'd wake up to Rege Cordic at five o'clock, before he took his surreal humour and cast of made-up characters and fake ads to the big-time in LA. Another Pittsburgh genius lost. I'd roll out of bed, pull in the stack of *Post-Gazettes,* and start folding them while putting tea water on to boil. By five-thirty, I'd have them stuffed into my delivery bag with its red tape reflectors. And then, out into the predawn air, forty minutes of imaginative mastery of my neighbourhood, the only person out and about, the Paul Revere of Pittsburgh bringing the news to houses where lights were just going on.

Now, as I walk through a commercial forest of defunct kitchen technologies, it feels as though the airport curator has trawled through my memories, the late forties and early fifties, the age of faith in plastic, fibreglass and chlorophyll. My memories have become museum-quality. Mixmasters, Osterizers, Sunbeams, Emersons, juicers, mixers, squeezers, peelers, dicers, raspers, openers, sealers, the first clock radio, first electric coffee-maker, a shoe-buffer, the first power toothbrush, the first hair-dryer, the first home permanent, a nozzle attachment to the garden hose for power car-washing, rabbit ears, bow-tie antennas and a television magnifier. Dead ends or missing links? When, or where? Hard to know.

And then it hit. On a bottom shelf labelled '1935', something intimately familiar snagged my eye. The round chromium waffle-maker had been my parents' mid-Depression wedding present. Four reversible surfaces, one side smooth for pancakes and grilled cheese sandwiches, the reverse cleated for waffles, and I'm suddenly overcome. I remember smells, the odour of burning butter, browning batter, the blistering of banana slices and blueberries, the hot chrome and the heating element, the bare wires, the holes in the insulating sleeve. I stare at the waffle-maker, expecting the lid to rise and yellow liquid to run down its sides. I used to make myself waffles before setting out with my papers. The frayed cord should have burst into flame. I remember the yellow strands of batter escaping from the rising lid and running in liquid tongues down the sides, bubbling and growing dull as they toasted and solidified and finally turned brown.

And suddenly, I remember a slim arm reaching, delicate fingers peeling off the browned, hardened lava flows of batter and the flattened cheese sandwich and the distant sound of bangles jangling, and in what others might have interpreted as pain, I cry out, *Laxmi!*

3. Lost in Space

First class, of course. Champagne flows. I close my eyes and fall half-asleep, papers on my lap. I wake for a second champagne, but we're still on the ground. An hour later, we take off. The day has already been eventful and the sun has just begun to rise.

By the time I was twelve, I'd attended the births of five brothers and sisters. Each baby had a name and a room and piles of appropriate-coloured clothing. Each inhabited a biography of my invention, and they still do. I'd felt their kicks and believed my mother when she swore that *this* time, from any of a dozen subtle hints – the kicks had been stronger or aimed from a different angle, there'd been more (or less) morning sickness, and she'd gained less (or more) weight – it would turn out differently. Three were stillborn, two survived a day, and all were eventually dropped into the hospital's trash. My mother believed her womb to be a poisoned place.

Fifty years ago, every birth – the sex, the abnormalities – arrived as a surprise. When my wild, brilliant brother and beautiful, talented sister, the two who made it out of the delivery room, had been properly wrapped and placed in a bassinet behind the maternity ward glass, 'Baby Morris' didn't need to be pointed out. In my family, first impressions were usually the last. They didn't kick or cry, they stared back with slate-blue eyes as though they had already passed judgement on this world and opted directly for the next. A nurse hovered in the background, showing the baby, then carrying it away. Death was only a few hours away.

I'm the most densely populated only child in the world. I've had the company of my brothers and sisters every minute of my days and nights. Their lives continue in my head, they are the stuff of the films I write. By fifteen, I didn't have a teenager's lust to rebel, but rather, to brother. I had no exploitable talent – no showy gifts, no agility, no voice, and no shamelessness in public. I had traces of the same genetic mismatch that had killed my siblings, a complicated set of conditions I'd survived merely by being my mother's first pregnancy. A doctor told me, 'You're on a long fuse. Who knows when it will run out?'

In the Pittsburgh ninth grade, while my classmates mesomorphed by the day, my body grew softer and more pliant. I could have slept through every day after delivering my morning papers. My eyes felt like radishes, red and bulbous, and the effort to keep them open consumed my daylight hours. At night, fears of not ever waking kept me awake. Thyroid collapse, the doctors said, prescribing the latest pills. (I'm still on them.) They hinted that I might be headed for sideshow freakishness, a grotesque, five-hundred-pound adulthood alleviated by an early death.

Our bodies were changing, and so was the school population. The local Catholic school went only to the eighth grade. In ninth grade, we got their graduates, to the joy of the football coach and the torment of boys like me. Kids I'd known all my life were becoming tight-sweatered girls smoking outside the school, or the rumble-voiced boys clustered around them. They, at least, ignored me. I was their alien familiar, their slightly crazy classmate with the famous father. But on a deeper, slower, less spectacular level, my hormones were doing their heroic best.

It started at a soda fountain near my house, and the young woman named Wanda who dipped ice cream with her top buttons undone. She was tall and solid, with bleached hair pulled high, then falling down in ringlets. Her sandwiches came with a residue of tobacco smell, and occasional specks of thick make-up that fell on the plate. Who could resist such a vision? When she dipped ice cream, I leaned forward, dazzled by the tubs of pastel colour and the deep cleavage, growing ever darker as she undid a second button. 'You want another dip?' she'd ask, 'it'll cost you.'

Thuggish Catholics took over the soda fountain. They reached across the counter, down into those dark crevices. 'Two giant scoops of vanilla,' they'd order, 'with cherries. Big red ones.' It took me a few days to understand why she dipped and why they reached, but no ice cream was ever served. Three pairs of arms fed on her bosom like a litter of snakes. 'Yeah, Morris, whatchalookin at, ya christkillin sheenie? Wouldntcha like some? Wouldntcha like a little squeeze ... like this?' 'Hey, watch it, asshole,' she'd snap. She was growing fatter by the week. In the beginning, she was able to wear street clothes under her uniform, then, in her full glory she could barely fit into her uniform at all. She changed in the storage room, sometimes with the door just slightly ajar.

I was putting down fifty cents a time for dipping rights. One dip or two? You want the cherry too? 'Only cherry here's Morris,' the boys would leer, their honking voices, the cupped cigarettes, flicking their fingers over the glowing ash. I could spend my entire paper route money on visits to Wanda, or in the dark supply room when she'd hover by the half-opened door, amidst the gallon jars of maraschino cherries, mayonnaise and mustard. She was even wider than I was, but patient as I fumbled the buttons, a dollar got her bottom buttons, too. For five dollars, the rumour went, she'd pick you up and stuff you in.

Out the window, I make out Mono Lake, or maybe Tahoe. Why, of all things in my life, these memories now? I'm going to New York, not Pittsburgh. Wanda is probably dead. Most of those high school tormentors, smokers, risk-takers, drop-outs, are probably dead. And here is Lew Morrison: sixty, reasonably fit, terrors behind him, with a fresh glass of champagne on his armrest.

4. Juliet of the Spirits

When I turned sixteen, I would drive out to the Greater Pittsburgh International Airport just to feel connected to a wider world and to watch glamorous people coming and going. Anyone getting on a California flight or arriving from New York was by definition glamorous. The airport earned its international status by hosting Mexican, Jamaican and Toronto flights twice a week. Shops and restaurants lined the concourses like an underground fantasy. It didn't seem possible that Pittsburgh people actually went to fabled places like Los Angeles, or that Pittsburgh could attract people with better places to have come from. They deplaned like Hollywood stars or politicians expecting a crowd, standing briefly at the top of the stairs. Every passenger could believe himself, briefly, a celebrity.

That was the year, 1956, when in a moment of inspiration I prevailed upon my parents one final time for a sibling. A ready-made contemporary, in the form of an exchange-brother for the year. I'd settled on saying a brother only because of the shame of really wanting a sister.

A German boy answered the call – why had I begged for such a fate? In movies and television shows, Germans were still the incarnate evil. My mother, whose background was German and Irish, seemed happy enough. His name was Heinz, not the best name for Pittsburgh, especially as he'd belong to the class of '57, so he agreed to being called Hank for the year. Hank was blond and robust. Soccer balls figured prominently in the photos he sent, his foot planted upon them, as team captain. I wrote two fluent, rather formal letters, adopting a slightly conspiratorial, brotherly tone, while dodging the request for a picture. My mother called her oldest relatives, collecting recipes and scraps of remembered German. I assured Hank about the ease of American schoolwork, especially for someone who had studied English for ten years, Greek and Latin and French for five, as well as college level math and physics. When he asked about football, I knew what he meant, but sent back a Steelers brochure. Out in private schools in Shadyside or Fox Chapel, soccer and lacrosse must have been played, but not anywhere I'd ever gone, nor by anyone I'd ever met.

He would have a bedroom to himself – freshly painted and decorated with Frederick Remington prints. The house smelled of sauerkraut. On a late August evening we drove out to the airport, carrying flowers to meet my brother's New York flight. And we waited, checking the faces against Hank's photo, then checking the flight manifest and waiting around the airport until the corridors and waiting areas cleared.

The only other person in the waiting area was a dark-skinned girl in a colourful, sarong-style wrap, something from *over there* without a name in those years, in that place. She'd been sitting in the corner staring at the wall holding a flimsy bag, but after an hour I could see she'd started crying very quietly. My father was impatient to get home, my mother almost broken-hearted – was there no end to the numbers of children taken from her? I took the bouquet to the girl and asked, 'Are you expecting someone?' For the first time in my life, I felt that a girl was looking first at my face, and not at my body. I did not expect her to comprehend English. Her dark brown eyes, edged in black, were larger, Disney-larger, than any eyes I had ever seen.

I couldn't bear to look at her. The singularity of her beauty, if it was that, wiped out any notice of individual features. I couldn't assess; I had no training. No one in Pittsburgh had ever seen a young woman from India. For many years, I have stared long and hard into roses and into the bougainvillea that clings to my cottage, into colours so intense they lack all dimension, colours so strong my eyes water, I can understand tumbling into them, like a bumblebee. The eyes, the full mouth and unblemished skin, a fine gold chain, gold earrings and gold bangles on her wrist, and now the bouquet of flowers against her sari – it was overwhelming, unfair, for a Pittsburgh boy. I knew she was beautiful, and I knew that no one else would get beyond the strange clothes and dark skin to find her so.

'I am waiting for Mr and Mrs Morris and their son, Lewis,' she said. Her voice was deep, her accent very British. She held out a carefully folded letter. 'You must be Lewis. My name is Laxmi.'

On the drive home my mother said, 'You must be so hungry after such a trip,' as though she had come directly from India, a week without a break. India and all it represented – poverty and starvation, Nehru's leadership, or the moral persuasion of Mahatma Gandhi – were as remote from my mother's consciousness as celestial mechanics. She asked if Laxmi liked Wiener schnitzel, which even then was warming on a hot-tray waiting its final topping of lemon butter. 'I'm sure I will,' she said, 'thank you.' After a pause she asked, casually, what exactly Wiener schnitzel was, in order that she might send the recipe home. I watched her face as my mother began describing pork tenderloin dredged in egg yolks and flour, then fried. Her voice never wavered. 'That would be from the flesh of pigs?' she asked, and I knew immediately she was vegetarian, a concept I'd never entertained, but one that suddenly seemed accessible and appealing.

'I don't think Laxmi eats meat,' I piped up, to which my mother responded, 'Then whatever would she eat?' I saw myself eating nothing but Wheaties with sliced bananas, whole dinners of salads and vegetables, growing lean and releasing the athlete within. She loved our home, the game room and trophy case. She knew Gene Kelly from musicals she'd watched every week in Calcutta. 'Calcutta!' my mother shuddered. 'You poor thing.' She loved her room with its musky cowboy motif, and immediately began transforming it. The Remington prints were replaced with paintings of blue-skinned babies and multi-armed women with a bloody tongues and necklaces of severed heads. What kind of monster had we admitted to our family? She arranged her dresser-top with brass gods and crushed flowers, and silver-framed portraits of her parents, who seemed almost normal. 'Just a few needful ornaments,' she said, as though quoting a distant author in order to placate the panic on my mother's face.

Within the week came a letter from Hank, now restored to Heinz, notifying his American parents and brother that at the last moment and under an urgent deadline he had accepted a soccer scholarship to an eastern prep school. My mother's last hope and my last fear had vanished. Confirmation came from Washington that the alternate, Laxmi Vinodbhavan of Calcutta, India, the first Indian ever selected, was their exchange scholar.

Who needed Rege Cordic? I awoke without the radio. However quiet my steps downstairs, she would be waiting for me in the kitchen. 'Will banana slices be all right, Lewis?' she'd ask, or would I prefer slices of strawberries, or blueberry chunks? The batter hissed as it covered the greased cleats, then worked its way like a yellow flood through the hot metal stumps. A nutty aroma burst from the magic machine, the top lifted, creamy rivulets snaked down its side, hissing and browning before they reached the counter. She made tea. The evolving gentleman, I poured the second round of batter, scraping the last lumpy drops from the mixing bowl, and she took it away for cleaning. It was, I realize now, the shortest, most perfect of my marriages. I drank my tea with milk, the way she taught me. We finished the waffles, light on syrup, heavy on fruit, then picked up our coats and gloves from the pegs behind the door and set out together delivering the *Post-Gazettes* deep in the winter dark.

Out the window, basin and range, Nevada, western Utah. Another champagne. I wanted the memories to stop. I knew where they were heading.

'Vegetarian, Dr Thampi?' the flight attendant asked and an Indian voice at my elbow, a seat companion who'd slipped in as I half-slept, said, 'Yes, thank you, madam.'

'And Mr Morrison. Wow! Two vegetarians in one row.'

'Keeps us hale and healthy, isn't it?' Dr Thampi said with the conspiratorial wink of a fellow veggie. Many years had passed, and many Indian seatmates, and I still expected some day she'd show up in an airport waiting room, or on my plane, or in the vast shopping areas of Heathrow or Frankfurt. For forty years I have been listening for her name, and taking a second look at Indian women my age, until the Indian population grew too large and varied. I didn't even know her married name. I'd spent a lifetime denying the very possibility that she was dead or no longer the person I remembered.

5. The Cyrano of Mt. Lebanon High

Legal and scientific niceties aside, Laxmi's skin was not white, which in those times and in that place qualified her for avoidance, and me for special attention. My locker developed a propensity for sandwich butts, banana skins and cartons of milk stuffed or poured through the gill slits. My combination lock froze under daily coats of nail polish and squirts of glue. Soon, emissions were noted, neighbouring lockers had to be emptied. The school assigned demerits and service charges for having to saw away three combination locks. I served my after-school punishment in the principal's outer office, doing my added homework assignments then reading my way through the library's modest holdings of fiction and history. I didn't mind the delay. The reprieve from walking through the knots of tormentors was worth the fines and added assignments. And Laxmi waited with me, devouring the library and answering her parents' daily letters. The existence of an 'American literature' apart from Mark Twain had been an unsustainable rumour in her Calcutta convent school.

My mother's prayers had landed her with a black-skinned polytheist who dressed like Maria Montez, ate only fruits and vegetables, worshipped monkeys and elephants and hung disgusting paintings on her walls. And worse, she feared, she was out to seduce her husband and son.

It came to pass in my eleventh grade that the state board of education decreed *Romeo and Juliet* to be that year's required Shakespeare text. The idea of adolescents dying for love, arranging midnight trysts and defying parental authority posed predictable demands from the adventurous for less hypocrisy, and from parents for its immediate suppression. We'd barely survived the previous year's mention of fairies in *A Midsummer Night's Dream*. Only a thuggish Catholic could shuffle to the head of the class and read the lines of Oberon.

It happened that Laxmi's convent school in Calcutta had prepared her so well in *Romeo and Juliet* that she required no text. She had acted as Romeo in the sixth grade and as Mercutio in the seventh and finally as Juliet in the ninth. Her eighth and tenth years had been given over to Gilbert and Sullivan and two of the history plays.

'I beg your pardon?' It was Dr Thampi, removing his headphones. 'Were you speaking to me?' His smile was benign and genuine.

'Sorry if I was mumbling,' I apologized. 'I'm trying to remember some lines and it helps to say them aloud.'

'Oh, don't I know! I acted a bit myself, in my younger years.'

The in-flight movie was one I'd doctored, coming in late for a top fee and no credit. I could remember Shakespeare from forty-five years ago, but not my own words of the year before.

'Macbeth was my headiest role,' said Dr Thampi. 'My parents were afraid for a few months that I might be lost to medicine.'

On any other day except this one, which seemed increasingly enchanted, I might have engaged my seatmate, might have spoken of my own Shakespearean experience. 'You wouldn't be from Calcutta, would you?' I asked.

The doctor seemed to giggle. 'No, no. My parents came to Bombay from the south. I am flattered you think me Bengali. Calcutta is a very Shakespearean city, you know.'

'I had an old friend from Calcutta, that's all.'

He nodded, apparently satisfied. *Enjoy the movie,* I wanted to say. A few seconds later he said, 'Bengali women are most enchanting, are they not?'

It shows? 'How's the movie?'

'A bit slow for my tastes. Too much talk.'

She said once, *My father's from the south, but my mother's Bengali. They met in England and thought they'd never go back. Then it wouldn't be so bad.*

'What's so bad?' I'd asked, wanting to say everything about you is perfect.

Being a mutt. 'Culturally displaced' they said. That's why they thought going to America would do me good. Over there, no one knows a thing about us. You're an ambassador from an unexplored kingdom.

'Do you know the name Vinodbhavan?' I asked.

'It is definitely not a Bengali name,' said Dr Thampi. "Bhavan" means house. House of Vinod. In medical school, I knew one.'

As the dawn approached and our papers were all delivered, Laxmi would turn to the east where half the night's stars had disappeared and cry out, *Give me my Romeo, and when he shall die take him and cut him out in little stars, and he will make the face of Heaven so fine that all the world will be in love with night and pay no worship to the garish sun.*

And I, to her: *Famine is in thy cheeks, Need and oppression starveth in thine eyes, Contempt and beggary hangs upon thy back.*

'Another waffle, is it?'

Oh, Laxmi and Lew brought something to Pittsburgh never before seen or heard. In the early weeks under her spell, with half the day's calories ingested before the sunrise and unaccustomed bursts of exercise, no stops for Cokes or double vanilla dips at Wanda's counter, the pounds were dropping away. My body slimmed from bulbous to tubular.

6. The Romeo and Juliet of Mt. Lebanon High School

'Class,' said their teacher on the first day of the Shakespeare unit, 'it's important to realize that this couple were children no older than you.' She was the last of the old-fashioned schoolmarms: severe, censorious, but when it came to Shakespeare, smitten and sentimental. Every word was brilliant, every scene perfect. The class of '57 had contained a number of promising Romeos and Juliets, but by the eleventh grade most of the red-hot lovers had dropped out and been forced into marriage. When the time came to allocate parts for the classroom reading, the choice of attractive, literate candidates had dwindled to a handful. I had been reading ahead for the Friar's role. Laxmi hadn't read at all, not wishing to reveal her expertise. 'Class, I want you to *feel* the language of Shakespeare. It doesn't matter who reads the words, what they look like, who they are – the language will transport us. For Juliet, then, I choose Laxmi.'

Predictable groans, some laughter. 'Hey, Ex-Lax,' the thuggish Catholics started.

She stood in her full red sari, faced them, and sweetly smiled. And in her Britishy alto, turning back to the teacher and without her book, she said, *It is an honour I dream not of ...*

'Act 1, scene 3,' said the teacher, holding back her astonishment.

'And for Romeo, who else but Lewis Morris?'

Shee-nee, Shee-nee, the same boys started, but I had no way of silencing them. Proud of my new body, proud of wearing khakis instead of my shiny gabardines, I knew, upon standing, they'd see (and I'd feel) my old pear shape. Some Romeo. Some anything. My blood ran cold, I wanted to run. Laxmi came to my desk, curtsied before me and took my hand as simply as a folded paper, or a washed dish passed to dry. She led me to the front, the voices mounted in the rear, Ex-Lax, Ex-Lax, She-nee, She-nee, and she turned again, our hands locked: *Good pilgrim,* she said, *you do wrong your hand too much ...* and at that moment, as though a prompter had cued me from behind a curtain, I said, *Have not saints lips, and holy palmers too?*

An inner voice went off, like words from a long-dead brother. *If you don't go through with this, you're finished. You may as well quit everything. You're all pretension.*

'Laxmi, where is your book? Don't tell me you've lost it.'

'I'm sorry. I did not think it was required.'

Until that day in the eleventh grade, playing Romeo in a Pittsburgh school with an Indian Juliet, I'd had no idea what my life would hold. Like all moderately bright boys from inland cities in the 1950s, I knew that science alone conferred respect. Until that day, if asked, I would have answered Geology or maybe Archaeology. But watching the teacher, as she lowered her book and raised her eyes to watch us, and then, the slow silencing of the restless boys, the smiles of girls who'd never noticed me, I knew what I was capable of and what I had to do.

One day, walking to school, she said, 'My poor Romeo. Do you know how appropriate this play is?' I replied that I thought I knew, not daring, in Cyrano-fashion, to leap over the hedges or spin through the ice-covered puddles like Gene Kelly in the rain. What could it mean but that my daily, hourly presence in her life had worked its magic, my essential kindness, even my nobility in rising to her standards and not falling to those around me had not gone unnoticed. And now, it had not gone unrewarded. I wanted to take her hand, to kiss it, to throw my arms around her. I, Lew Morris, no longer fat, no longer lost in the world, was writing plays during my after-school detention. I auditioned for a role in 'Our Town' and won it. There were no Indian parts for Laxmi. And now I had found my Roxanne, my love, and soon, very soon, it would be time, unlike my favourite hero, Cyrano, to break my silence. Oh, yes, I dared to answer; I know what you mean. What else could it mean?

At my elbow, I could feel Dr Thampi laughing out loud. And not just the good doctor, but others in the cabin. I have brought some laughter to the world. Not a small thing, I would plead.

6. My Father in Love

One dark, winter night in the silence of still-falling snow, I heard distant, familiar music and for a moment thought I was a child again, before the paper route, before Laxmi, before my self-election to the status of Romeo and Cyrano de Bergerac, when my father would rehearse his songs and dance steps in front of the Gene Kelly poster. It was three o'clock and my father no longer sang or danced, he rehearsed his routines with Mister Foystinger in the daytime. I made my way down to the game-room stairs. Tap-dancing crackled in the still winter air.

'This is the basic step,' I could hear. 'See, I keep the beat with my left

foot, like your left hand on the piano. Now, with my right – *here,* see?'
and for a crazy moment I thought the old gang had descended, Perry
and Gene and Dean had followed him home from a bar or a retreat. I did
not expect the dainty applause. My father was performing, for my Juliet,
my Roxanne, for the girl who burned with love for me and only me, and
I rose from my hidden place on the stairs and confronted them, not
knowing what to expect.

Laxmi was sitting in a leather chair. What she was wearing under her
bathrobe I couldn't tell. My father was in his television tux, minus the
jacket, with the ruffled shirt and cummerbund, the suspenders, the
black pants with the satin stripe, the glistening patent leather shoes.

'Was I too loud, son?'

Laxmi had been crying.

'I'm trying to cheer up our little girl.'

'Daddy-Lou is being very kind. I've been so silly,' she said. My father
lifted the phonograph needle, cutting the music.

'How could you be silly?'

'She's leaving us, son.'

'Parting is –' she said, and I dutifully followed, ' – such sweet sorrow.'

'Shakespeare is a fool. Parting is terrible sorrow,' she said. She held a
balled-up blue aerogramme. 'You've been very kind. I cannot tell you
how much these months have meant to me.' She smiled a complicated,
womanly smile that I had seen only in movies. She motioned me closer,
touched my cheek. '*O, that I were a glove upon that hand, that I might
touch that cheek.* I will never forget our waffles in the morning. I will
remember our paper route as long as I live. I will be the only girl in India
who can fold a newspaper tight enough to throw.'

She held my heart in her hand. 'Laxmi, what have we done?'

'She's getting married, son.'

'My parents say here,' she shook the letter, 'he is a good man,' she
said. 'My parents say he is well established. His first wife died and his
children need a mother. He is a man from the south, from our caste, our
families know one another. He will overlook the impurities of my
background. My parents' love-match is no impediment. Our
horoscopes match. All the needful particulars of my life are settled
nicely.'

'What are you talking about?'

'She's foreign, son.'

In *Romeo and Juliet* the role of Paris, Juliet's arranged groom, had been read by my worst antagonist, one of the regulars at Wanda's counter. The teacher had asked us, what do we think of arranged marriages? We'd all laughed, and then Laxmi had spoken up for the first time. 'What is wrong with parents arranging a marriage? How can I make an intelligent selection when they know so much more than I?'

'Let us look after you,' I begged. 'He's old, you don't have to leave us – Dad, make her stay!'

'It's in the agreement. We're not her parents.' He, too, had been crying.

Marry her! I thought, ask her now! Save both our lives! I tried to speak but no words, none of the golden words that had become our secret language poured out. My Romeo needed his Cyrano.

'They sent me the ticket. The wedding is next week, and you're all invited.'

She raised her hand to my cheek, then kissed me there, nothing passionate although it burned against the iciness I felt. 'He says I must leave school immediately. Please don't worry, I'll be well looked after.'

My father climbed down from his little stage in front of the ever-smiling Gene Kelly. Laxmi had already disappeared up the stairs. I turned off the downstairs lights. 'She's not foreign,' was all I could say: she's my sister, she's my Juliet, my love, and she's the closest, most familiar thing in my life. Because of her, my life makes sense, I'm a new person.

In the dark, he laid his arm over my shoulders. His hand was heavy and he pulled me closer to him. For a moment we stared at each other levelly. He was suddenly smaller than I thought; we were the same height. Then he threw his arms around me and I could feel his body shaking. I'd never seen my father cry, never heard his voice rise to a high, almost childish pitch.

'I tried everything. Forgive me, son.'

7. My Brothers Werner and Heinz

At JFK, a particle stands in the giant hangar-like structure, a particle roaming in the void, making its way to the escalators. A rank of taxis waits at the door. New York beckons as never before. But another sign attracts me: TICKETS it says. I am dealing with a fact that now blinds me with its luminescence, its obviousness. Whatever honours and pleasures I have known, the ephemeral body of profitable work, do not rank with predawn waffle making when I was sixteen years old in my father's house in a city I haven't seen in thirty years. My life has been a one-way dialogue with a girl I never knew, whose marriage I never attended, name I no longer know, who might not remember me, whose address I don't know, who might even be dead.

Listen to me, Werner Heisenberg! The contingencies of sixty years are collapsing. I know when, and I know where; I refute uncertainty. It's a dialogue, this play of mine; two characters on stage, not just the physicist, but the playwright. Not just Heisenberg in the fatal, tragic certainty of his uncertainty, but the struggle of the creator to right an original wrong.

I hear myself saying, 'I want to go to India.'

'You're lucky, we have space today.' The woman flips through my passport. 'I can't sell you a ticket without a visa,' she says.

I want to say, God in heaven, woman, my whole life has been one long visa application, just give me the goddamn ticket! I want to mess up all the predictable patterns of my life. Oh, it's all suddenly so clear! In that, I will find my certainty. But I am the ever gracious, sixty-year-old, smiling, public man and some displays would be unseemly.

'I have a suggestion. You fly me to Frankfurt today, or London or Paris or Berlin, let me lay over for a day, and I'll get a visa tomorrow.'

'Works for me,' she giggles. 'We can do that.'

She stares at me just a little too long. 'You really mean it, don't you, sir?'

Acknowledgements

A number of the stories included here have been previously published: 'The Birth of the Blues' appeared in *Lusts* (1983); 'Identity' appeared in *Resident Alien* (1986); 'Grids and Doglegs' and 'The Seizure' appeared in *Tribal Justice* (1974); and 'Dunkelblau' and 'Snake in Flight over Pittsburgh' appeared in *Man and His World* (1992).

Several of the stories were included in the following magazines or anthologies: 'The Unwanted Attention of Strangers' in *The New Quarterly;* 'Dunkelblau' in *The Workshop;* and 'Sitting Shivah with Cousin Benny' in *Salmagundi.* 'The Waffle Maker' will be published in an upcoming issue of *The Michigan Quarterly Review.*